AN ACT OF LOVE

A diamond brooch is the only clue Abbie Rogers has to her own identity ... and her quest to find her real mother leads her to glamorous actress Diana LaTrobe and the exotic Foxton family. Unaware of the mystery behind Abbie's past, Diana asks Abbie to stay and help her write her memoirs. Amongst the memorabilia Abbie finds the answers to some of her questions, and the reason why she must not fall in love with Diana's son Sim ...

MARGARET MOUNSDON

AN ACT OF LOVE

Complete and Unabridged

LINFORD
Leicester

First published in Great Britain in 2009

First Linford Edition
published 2011

British Library CIP Data

Mounsdon, Margaret.
   An act of love. - -
   (Linford romance library)
   1. Birthparents- -Identification- -Fiction.
   2. Actresses- -Fiction. 3. Autobiography- -
   Authorship- -Fiction. 4. Romantic suspense
   novels. 5. Large type books.
   I. Title II. Series
   823.9′2–dc22

   ISBN 978–1–44480–529–1

Published by
F. A. Thorpe (Publishing)
Anstey, Leicestershire

Set by Words & Graphics Ltd.
Anstey, Leicestershire
Printed and bound in Great Britain by
T. J. International Ltd., Padstow, Cornwall

This book is printed on acid-free paper

Abbie Meets The Famous Diana

'Darling,' Diana trilled at Abbie as she flung open the back door. 'You're awfully late, but never mind.'

A blast of warm air hit Abbie in the face as she peered at the woman silhouetted in the doorway. Even if she had wanted to back out, it was too late now. The only way was forward.

'Er, hello,' she began, 'I'm sorry I didn't get here earlier.'

'You're here at last and that's all that matters.'

'Yes, I . . . '

'Honestly, trust my mother to let us down and on an atrocious night like this. What a time to take her bike to Beach Brow, or wherever it is she's gone. It's time she remembered her age, although that's actually something

1

I don't usually go on about too much. People might work out how old I am if I let on how old Molly is.' This last remark was delivered with a girlish laugh.

Abbie continued to blink at the beautiful woman standing in front of her. She knew from her research that Diana LaTrobe admitted to fifty-nine but was actually sixty-five.

'Come in. Come in. Don't know why Johnny insists on going out on a filthy night like this. I'd much rather stay in and have something light on a tray.'

'I'm sorry, Mrs Foxton, but your instructions were a little — er, vague,' Abbie apologised, feeling as though she had been hit by a whirlwind.

'Call me Diana, please.' Her voice was light and full of laughter. 'I'm only Mrs Foxton to the bank manager, and then only when I am seriously overdrawn,' she leaned forward confidentially, 'which is practically all the time I'm ashamed to admit. He's such a tedious little man and so small.'

Diana made a gesture of irritation, 'but what on earth are we doing standing on the doorstep discussing the bank manager? You're absolutely soaked to the skin. Come along inside and dry off.'

'Thank you.' Laden down with laptop and overnight bag, Abbie staggered into the kitchen, which was a blaze of warmth and light after the darkness outside.

'What lovely hair.' Diana helped her out of her coat as Abbie shook the raindrops off her auburn locks. 'With that colouring you must be Celtic — such lovely pale skin, too.'

Abbie still could not quite believe she was actually here. Standing in front of her smiling and looking impossibly glamorous as one of the most famous actresses of her generation. Her eyes, which the camera and fans absolutely adored were a mesmeric greeny blue. Until now Abbie had always suspected they were touched up, but here under the harsh kitchen lighting she realised

3

she was wrong. Diana LaTrobe was a truly beautiful woman. With her flawless complexion and classic bone structure she did not need cosmetic enhancement. She was quite simply stunning.

'I see you've brought your overnight case.' Diana eyed Abbie's holdall. 'What a sensible thing to do. Johnny and I will probably be back late and you're most welcome to sleep over.'

The kitchen was a huge Victorian room with lots of pantry doors and a high-beamed ceiling from which dangled a mixture of garlic, onions, dried herbs and a rather dangerous looking ham. It swayed to and fro as Diana battled against the wind and rain to close the door.

'Filthy night. Who would believe it was April? It's more like November outside. There, all safe and warm.' Several diamond rings sparkled off Diana's perfectly manicured fingers as she gestured an elegant hand towards a small figure standing by a huge pine table. 'This is Bethan, your charge for the evening. Bethan is making beans on toast. I expect you'd like something to eat too after your journey? Bethan, sweetheart, come and meet — I'm sorry,' Diana turned back to Abbie, 'I've completely forgotten your name. I know I should remember it but after a lifetime of learning scripts, now I've retired I've rather lost the knack. I've tried word association but it doesn't work and you have to be very careful you don't put your foot in it when you play that game. I mean if someone has bushy eyebrows I'm quite likely to say, 'Hello Mrs Eyebrows,' or something dreadful like that,' Diana's tinkling laughter faded into a frown as she took a closer look at Abbie.

'I'm sorry I'm making a mess on your floor, er, Diana,' Abbie looked down in dismay to where a puddle of water was forming around her feet. Rain was still dripping off the hem of her trousers.

Diana dismissed her apology with a

shake of her head.

'Forgive me for being rude but haven't we met before Miss er . . . ?'

Abbie stiffened. 'I don't think so.' She cleared her throat to ease the tightness threatening to lock her vocal chords. 'And it's Abbie, Abbie Rogers.'

'Of course.' Diana stepped backwards uncertainly. She was still frowning and looked confused. 'I'm not very good with names, but faces I never forget and I could have sworn we had definitely met somewhere before.'

'I don't think we move in the same social circles.' Abbie did her best to keep her reply light-hearted.

'Probably not.' Diana hesitated. 'Have you ever been to . . . '

'So you're here at last.' A male voice boomed from the doorway into the hall and a dinner-suited silver haired man bustled into the kitchen.

'Is this the girl?' he asked then reeled back as Abbie flicked more damp hair away from her face and smiled at the new arrival.

'Hello, I'm Abbie Rogers.'

She wasn't sure she liked being referred to as the girl but until she found out the exact status in the household of the man standing in front of her, she decided to keep her opinion to herself.

'Good heavens,' he said, 'er, yes. Quite.'

He extended a hand in greeting to Abbie and crushed her fingers. 'Johnny Cavendish, pleased to meet you.' The bushy eyebrows relaxed their frown. 'Now, Dee are we ready to go? The babysitter is here. Bethan's got supper sorted. You're all tricked out in your glad rags.'

'Doesn't Abbie remind you of someone, Johnny?' Diana asked.

'Never mind all that,' he began to hustle her towards the door.

'D . . . did you say babysitter?' Abbie stuttered but no one appeared to be paying any attention to her.

'Don't fuss, Johnny,' Diana complained, 'Abbie and I were getting to know each other. You wouldn't want me to leave Bethan in the care of a total stranger would you?'

'The agency will have seen to all the necessary security checks. Come on, Dee. We haven't got all night and it doesn't do for the guest of honour to be late.'

'Bethan will show you where everything is, Abbie.' Diana seemed reluctant to leave, but Johnny was having none of it as he ushered a still twittering Diana out of the kitchen.

'We'll be back about midnight,' he called out, 'and remember don't open the door to anyone. You get some funny people walking along the towpath at night. We've got our own keys so we can let ourselves in.'

'Where's my clutch bag?'

'Dee, will you please get a move on?'

Their voices faded down the corridor. Abbie looked helplessly after them until the smell of baked beans drew her attention back to the slender child standing by the cooker patiently stirring a saucepan.

'Hello,' she smiled shyly at Abbie, revealing teeth braces. 'They take a bit of getting use to, don't they?'

'You're Bethan?' Abbie asked.

'Yes. I thought I'd let Johnny get Diana out of the way before I introduced myself. Diana's my grandmother. She doesn't like to be called Granny or anything like that.' A dimple deepened Bethan's cheek. 'Do you know she tells everyone she is only fifty-nine?' she raised her eyebrows, 'as if.' She giggled. 'I really am eight years old.'

'And I, er,' Abbie smiled ruefully, 'have a confession to make.'

'You have?' Bethan looked intrigued.

'I'm not your babysitter.'

'Cool.' Bethan squeaked in delight, her huge blue eyes widening dramatically. 'Diana's really got it wrong this time, hasn't she?'

'Would you like me to call her back and explain?' Abbie offered.

'Johnny would go mental,' Bethan said after a moment's thought. 'He's a stickler for punctuality and it's his big night at the golf club. He's been trying to get Diana out of the house for over an hour.'

They heard the sound of a car starting up outside and tyres moving slowly over the gravel. 'Too late now anyway.' Bethan tasted her beans. 'They're done.' She looked at Abbie. 'You haven't come to rob us or anything have you?' she asked anxiously.

'No. I may not be the babysitter, but I'm not a burglar either.'

'That's OK, then. I don't think we've actually got much worth taking anyway, 'cept Diana's film stuff. Fancy some supper? Beans and a banana?'

Abbie's stomach rumbled at the thought of food. 'Delicious.'

All she'd had was a lukewarm motorway coffee about three hours earlier as she'd tried to unravel Diana's confusing directions for Hamwater.

'Do you need to freshen up? There's a washbasin in the cold room over there.' Bethan nodded to a door in the corner of the kitchen. 'I'll do the toast.'

Abbie Begins Her Quest

'So,' Bethan waved her fork at Abbie. 'If you're not the babysitter who are you?'

'I'm a freelance journalist.'

'Brilliant.' Bethan looked suitably impressed.

'And I've come to interview Diana for a colour supplement commission I'm doing on famous actresses of the seventies.'

'Gosh,' Bethan giggled. 'And Diana forgot you were coming?'

'Looks like it. I emailed confirmation this morning.'

'Molly does all that computer stuff for Diana, but she's gone off on her motorbike so I expect no one's read it yet.'

'Who is Molly?'

'She's my great grandmother, Diana's mother. She lives with us on and off when she and Diana are speaking. The rest of the time she lives on a houseboat moored on the river. The family's a bit complicated. I'll tell you about it later. Go on about your commission. What's it like being a journalist?'

Abbie looked into the young face. Bethan seemed a remarkably normal child considering her background. She also seemed rather grown up for her age, but Abbie supposed being Diana's granddaughter must have involved a certain amount of fending for herself.

'It's fun, sometimes more than others.'

'Have you interviewed anyone, like, famous?' Bethan asked.

Abbie named a couple of teen stars who had in her opinion been the dullest of her commissions, but Bethan looked excited.

'Wow,' she beamed at Abbie.

'Apart from that there's not much more to say about the job, really,' Abbie admitted. 'It's much like any other work. Sometimes it's fascinating, sometimes it's dull.'

'I wish you'd been here earlier, there's been no one to talk to all day,' Bethan complained. 'That's the trouble when you haven't got any brothers or sisters.'

'I would have been here earlier but I got lost after I left the motorway and there wasn't anyone about to ask for directions. I've run out of credit on my mobile, so I stopped at just about every petrol station going until I finally found Waterside Cottage. Now it seems I wasn't even expected.'

'Diana is always forgetting appointments.' Bethan confided as if they were sharing a huge joke. 'It drives her agent mad, but she gets away with it because she's — well beautiful. She gets away with everything,' Bethan ended on a rather forlorn note.

'Yes, she is beautiful,' Abbie agreed in a quiet voice, 'and I'm sure she does get away with things.'

'Hey, Abbie, what's with the serious?' Bethan joked. 'You will sleep over, won't you? I mean even if the real babysitter turns up?'

'If you want me to, I'll stay, but we can't dismiss the babysitter, it wouldn't be fair.'

'I 'spect she's lost as well if Diana gave her the same set of instructions. She wrote them out years ago, before the housing estate was built and she forgets things like roundabouts and new roads. Workmen are always getting lost. A lot of people give up.'

'That's a shame. Waterside Cottage is a lovely house,' Abbie said.

In the course of her research Abbie had looked up Diana on the internet. She had also read up on Waterside Cottage. It was a large family house and a fine example of 1930s architecture, situated down by the river with access from the water via a private landing stage. In its heyday it had been the centre for numerous studio parties and country house weekends.

'It looks better in the daylight,' Bethan said. 'Diana lived here with my grandfather and then her second husband, but I expect you know all that.'

Abbie nodded through a mouthful of beans. Her notes on the Foxtons were extensive and stretched back several generations. Diana's family had been the glamorous LaTrobes who'd been a constant feature in the gossip columns of the day. One had even married into minor foreign royalty and another had been awarded a medal for heroic wartime deeds.

'Do you live here all the time?' Abbie asked Bethan.

'Ever since Mummy died.' Bethan blinked. 'That was seven years ago. I was only a baby at the time. Daddy is Diana's younger son. He's away filming a lot and doesn't live here much. He does wildlife photography and travels all over the world. I'll show you a picture of him later. He's ever so handsome. Have you finished?'

Abbie put down her knife and fork. 'That was very good. Thank you.'

'I'm used to cooking things on toast.

Diana's not very good at domestic stuff. She often forgets meal times.'

'I can imagine.'

'But she's the best grandmother in the world,' Bethan added loyally.

Abbie smiled at the serious little face and tweaked one of Bethan's plaits.

'I'm sure she is and I'm sure she loves you.'

'Have you got a grandmother?'

'Not any more.'

Abbie didn't have parents either, but she decided the less Bethan knew about her personal life the better. Images of the vicarage in Devon with its tiny garden and cramped rooms flashed through her mind; her childhood had been idyllic and very different she imagined from Bethan's at Waterside Cottage.

There was nothing remotely glamorous about life at the vicarage, but every day had been filled with love and laughter.

'I'll show round tomorrow if you like.'

The wall telephone burst into life and Bethan leapt up to answer it.

'That's OK. No, it's fine really. Bye.'

She sat down again with a secret little smile on her lips.

'That was the real babysitter. She's not coming. So you are staying over aren't you, Abbie?' she asked.

'Do you think Diana will mind?'

'Course not. She never minds about anything and she loves having people to stay. Besides you haven't interviewed her yet. She'll take ages to get ready for that. You'll probably be here all next week. You've got time haven't you?'

'Well — er . . . '

'Please say you'll stay. It's nice to have someone to talk to. It gets a bit lonely at times, especially during school holidays. I ride my pony and take the dogs for a walk, but it's not the same is it?'

Two Labradors were stretched out in front of the boiler. They raised their heads at the mention of the word walk, then went back to their snooze, as

17

Bethan didn't appear to be making good on her promise.

'Who else lives here? Johnny?'

'No. He'd like to,' Bethan pushed a huge bowl of fruit towards Abbie.

Abbie picked up an orange and began to peel it.

'He's Diana's boyfriend, sort of. They've known each other for ages. Johnny wants to marry Diana. He's got a flat in the village. He drives a huge old fashioned saloon car. Did you see it outside?'

'I didn't see anything much in the wind and rain.'

'Sim calls him a poser, I don't know what that is,' Bethan admitted, 'but we all like Johnny. He's fun at parties and he's generous when it's your birthday. He gives me pocket money too.'

'Who's Sim?'

'He's my uncle. He works at the golf club. I expect that's where he is now, with his girlfriend. He doesn't live here but he's always staying over too.'

Abbie's research had revealed that Diana's two sons were from her first marriage to impresario, Don Foxton. After his untimely death, she'd married again to a cameraman called Barney Jones although she kept her first husband's name.

'You don't mind looking after me do you?' Bethan asked as she squirted washing up liquid over their dirty plates. 'We can play cards or something later if you like. And I'll make up a bed for you. We've stacks of spare rooms.'

Abbie picked up a tea towel. 'Of course I don't mind. Besides I can't leave you all alone can I, now you've told the real babysitter not to come?'

'I suppose you can't.' Abbie finished drying her hands. 'I know, Diana's got a lovely big box of chocolates by her bedside. Let's go and eat some, she won't mind. She's always on a diet. We can watch one of her old films if you like. Do you remember that television series, *Masquerade*? She was in it. She played Lady Alexandra. We've got all the episodes taped. Come on.' Bethan dragged Abbie's hand. 'This way.'

The library was tucked away down the end of the corridor. It was a family room with oak panelled walls and lined with leather bound books that looked as though they had never been disturbed.

The drapes were dark plum velvet with golden tassels and had been pulled against the night. In one corner of the room a golden shaded lamp cast a gentle glow over a huge writing desk.

The dogs ambled in behind Abbie and Bethan and settled themselves in front of the coal fire crackling in the hearth. Newspapers had been scattered around the floor and left where they had fallen.

'Actually, there's lots of family stuff here. Want to take a look while I go and find Diana's chocolates?' Bethan pulled out an embossed bound photograph album from one of the bookcases and thrust it at Abbie. 'You can look through this if you like. Won't be a tick.

When I come back I'll tell you who everyone is.'

Abbie's hands were trembling as she accepted the album from Bethan before she raced out of the room.

It had all been so easy. Diana had accepted Abbie without question and apart from that nasty moment in the kitchen when she thought they'd met before, everything had run like clockwork.

Was there a resemblance? Did Abbie look like her mother? Was she of Celtic origin? Abbie had absolutely no idea, but that was what she had come here to find out.

Abbie put down the album and very carefully drew a scarlet velvet pouch out of her pocket. A diamond brooch slid out and into the palm of her hand. The facets gleamed in the firelight — a five pointed star brooch on white gold. She knew every detail by heart she'd looked at it so often, yet it had only come into her possession relatively recently.

Her fingers traced the delicate intricacy of the jewellery. This brooch was her only clue as to who she really was.

'Where did you get that from?' Abbie hadn't heard Bethan come back into the room. Startled she spun round. It was too late to hide the brooch now. 'Sorry,' Bethan apologised, 'didn't mean to make you jump. Gosh, isn't it beautiful? Is it yours?'

'Yes,' Abbie's voice was husky, 'it's mine.'

'Who gave it to you?'

Abbie replaced it carefully in its pouch. 'I think it belonged to my mother.'

'I Thought Abbie Was A Babysitter'

The smell of bacon lured Abbie down the servants' back staircase. After one or two false starts she found her way to the kitchen. Waterside Cottage was bigger than any cottage she had ever known and everything looked so different in the daylight.

There were at least three floors and several bedrooms on each floor. The boards creaked alarmingly underfoot as Abbie crept along the rabbit warren of corridors trying to find the right staircase down to the kitchen.

It had been well after midnight when she had finally got to bed. There had been no sign of Diana and Johnny, so after making up a bed in one of the rooms under the eaves, Abbie had reluctantly put Diana's photograph album back in the bookcase.

She and Bethan had sat up watching several episodes of *Masquerade* and eating chocolates, until the child began yawning incessantly and Abbie realised guiltily that she was only eight years old and needed her sleep. After a brief tussle of wills, during which Bethan displayed a remarkable stubbornness alarmingly akin to Diana's, the child had kissed Abbie on the cheek and accepted defeat with good grace.

After she'd retired for the night, Abbie leafed her way through the photograph album, mostly pictures of family and actors whose faces she thought she recognised, before she too had succumbed to sleep.

And now it was the morning and Abbie's stomach fluttered at the prospect of the day in front of her. Would she be able to keep up the charade of only being here for an interview? Or would Diana suspect the real reason?

A glance out of a leaded light window revealed a newly rain washed lawn, spears of newly mown grass sparkled with droplets of morning dew and lead down to a diamond bright stretch of river. The water flowed gently upstream now the wind had died down and the rain clouds had given way to a kinder April sky.

Abbie let out a sigh of happiness. She could understand why Waterside Cottage had been such a magnet to Diana's London set. She'd read somewhere as part of her research that it wasn't unusual for her parties to last for several days.

Abbie glanced at her watch. It was way past nine o'clock and time to go in search of Diana. Abbie unlatched the kitchen door and pushed it open.

'Who on earth are you?'

A man dressed in a tight white T shirt and close fitting jeans was grilling bacon. The eyes challenging hers were golden brown and while not exactly unfriendly were far from welcoming. Abbie put a hand to her hair in an unconscious feminine gesture, then annoyed for caring what this man would think of her hastily scrunched ponytail, she challenged him with, 'I could ask you the same question.'

A look of surprise crossed his face as if he was not used to having his authority challenged.

'Then *I* will be polite enough to answer.' He emphasised the pronoun, an irony not lost on Abbie. 'I am Sim Foxton and this is my mother's house.'

So this was Sim Foxton, Diana's elder son. Abbie studied him for a further moment trying to remember what Bethan had told her about her Uncle Sim the previous evening.

'Abbie Rogers,' she was jolted into a reply by the enquiring expression in Sim's eyes. 'I stayed overnight.'

His look travelled up from her fatigue cargo pants to the crisp business shirt Abbie favoured.

'So, Abbie Rogers would you like a bacon sandwich?'

The question was not what Abbie had been expecting. She hesitated.

'If you're vegetarian we've got some muesli somewhere.'

'A sandwich will be fine,' she said, flashing him a smile.

It was a moment before he returned her smile. It totally transformed the harsh lines of his face.

'Sorry,' he apologised, 'I didn't mean to be rude. I know I should get used to it.'

'Used to what?' Abbie asked.

'Coffee?' He waved a pot at her. 'Just made a fresh brew.'

'Please.' Abbie sat down at the pine table and watched him fill her mug while she inhaled the smell of the rich deep roast beans.

'People I've never met before appearing at Diana's breakfast table,' he answered her question. 'You're not a relative are you?' Sim enquired.

'No,' Abbie answered quickly.

'That's good. They're always turning up out of the blue, claiming to be a long lost daughter or something and then trying to get money out of Diana.'

27

Abbie could feel the first wave of a flush beginning to stain her neck. Sim's words were uncomfortably close to the truth. 'If I didn't stop her, Diana would fall for every hard luck story going.'

'Does that worry you?' Abbie asked.

'Frankly yes. You see along with being her son, I'm also her accountant.'

'I thought Bethan said you worked at the golf club.'

'Part time. I do their accounts as well.' Sim frowned. 'Haven't we met somewhere before?'

Abbie flinched at the suddenness of the question and affected a light laugh. 'That's exactly what Diana said to me.'

'So you've met my mother?'

Sim placed a plate of toasted sandwiches down on the table and sat opposite Abbie.

'Last night. She and Johnny were on their way out to the golf club dinner.'

Sim took a healthy bite out of a sandwich and began chewing. 'Are you the babysitter who got lost?' he asked after he swallowed his mouthful.

'Bethan was telling me a garbled story about Diana giving you the wrong directions and poor old Johnny nearly bursting a blood vessel because he thought you weren't going to turn up.'

'Actually she never did, the real babysitter. She telephoned later to say she wasn't coming.'

'What?'

'It's a long story, but I'm not the babysitter,' Abbie confessed nibbling a corner of toast.

A suspicious shadow crossed Sim's face. 'You're not?'

'No.' Abbie shook her head. 'Sorry.'

'So we still don't know who you are.' The scepticism was back in his voice.

'I'm a freelance journalist.'

All traces of warmth disappeared from Sim's voice in an instant. 'Out to dig up more dirt on my mother?' he asked with an angry twist to his mouth.

'No,' Abbie protested.

'Because I can tell you right now it's all been done before and there's nothing new anyone in your profession can say that hasn't already been hacked to death. Everything you can possibly want to know about her is on her website. When will you people leave her alone?'

'If you'll give me a chance to explain,' Abbie began.

'No. You listen to me. Worming your way into the house under the guise of being a babysitter sets new standards even by those of your profession.'

'Now hold on a moment.' Abbie slapped her mug back down on the table. Coffee slopped over the side and on to the tablecloth. 'You're entitled to your opinion of journalists, but when you accuse me of employing base standards by using an innocent child to get a story, enough is enough. I've had some insults in my time, but that one takes the biscuit.'

'I'm not sure I shouldn't report you to the authorities.'

'Then report away,' Abbie raised her voice to compete with Sim's. 'My professional integrity is above reproach.

It wasn't my fault Diana mistook me for the babysitter and what was I supposed to do after she and Johnny had driven off? Perhaps you would have preferred it if I'd driven off as well and left Bethan all alone in the house? If you're so concerned about your niece's welfare why weren't you here looking after her instead of dancing the night away at a golf club ball? No, don't bother to answer that. Spending the night with adoring females must be a much better way of passing an evening than watching reruns of *Masquerade*.'

'And filching Diana's very expensive box of Belgian chocs.'

'What?'

Abbie's delicate stain of colour around her neck had erupted into a full-blown blush.

Sim leaned forward confidentially. He was smiling now. 'Found the empty box in the trash can. For such a slender girl you've got a very healthy appetite. Do you know the tip of your nose has gone quite pink? Does it always do that when you're angry?'

A sharp pain in Abbie's ribcage reminded her she had forgotten to breathe while she had been delivering her tirade. She took a few moments out to catch her breath as she glared at Sim. Amusement tugged at the corner of his mouth further infuriating Abbie.

'Don't you dare laugh at me.'

'And don't you dare throw that plate at me,' he retaliated.

'Children, children.'

A spare figure sporting huge horn rimmed spectacles and a shock of snowy white hair stumped into the kitchen. Abbie turned away from Sim and gaped at the elderly lady wearing leather trousers and a bright purple jumper.

'Stand up when your elders and betters come into the room,' she instructed Sim.

Sim rose reluctantly to his feet with a look of resigned indulgence. 'Good morning, Molly.' He kissed her on the cheek and stroked her soft hair tenderly.

'Is it?' she snapped back at him. 'From the raised voices I thought war had broken out. What's it about this time?'

The sharp blue eyes behind the spectacles turned their attention to Abbie.

'Hello. Don't know who you are but don't let my brute of a grandson bully you,' she said. 'From what I overheard you were giving as good as you got.'

'I was not bullying Ms Rogers,' Sim objected.

'Rogers?' Molly frowned. 'Are you that journalist who sent me an email? Come to do a piece on Diana for a quality colour supplement?'

'Yes.' Abbie couldn't resist casting a triumphant look in Sim's direction.

'Good. Glad you've arrived. Sorry I wasn't here to welcome you last night. I was otherwise engaged. Is Sim looking after you?'

'He's actually accusing me of having gained access to Waterside Cottage under false pretences and he's threatening to report me for unprofessional behaviour.'

'Just like the rest of them, got no sense. Men,' Molly dismissed the male sex with a shrug of her shoulders. 'Where's my cup of Earl Grey?'

'It's coming.'

Far from being outraged by this slur on his sex, the smile Sim turned on Molly was full of warmth, gentle good humour and love.

'And men are something you know all about, aren't they?' he teased her.

'One husband was enough for me, thank you very much,' Molly retaliated, 'unlike my daughter.'

Sim placed a tray of tea and some delicate slices of buttered white bread in front of Molly. The crusts had been cut off and beside the rose patterned plate were little pots of marmalade and blackcurrant jam.

'I trust everything is to your ladyship's satisfaction?' Sim gave a mock bow and produced a vase containing a pink rose, which he placed in front of Molly.

The leaves were tightly furled and bedecked with early morning dew. The fragrance reminded Abbie of her father's rose garden in their Devon vicarage. Roses were his passion and he too liked fresh flowers on the table for breakfast.

Molly's blue eyes softened. 'There was always a fresh rose on my breakfast tray every morning of my married life. My husband used to get up at dawn to pick it for me.' Her voice was husky with emotion. She smiled at Abbie. 'Now there was a man for you. You'd have liked my husband, everybody did.'

'I'm sure I would,' Abbie agreed desperately trying to remember which member of the LaTrobe clan Molly had married.

'Sir Justin knew how to flatter the ladies,' Sim said to Abbie.

'Of course,' Abbie made a gesture with her hands.

'Wassat?' Molly looked up from pouring tea into her bone china cup.

'Your husband was the motorbike racer.'

'He was a rogue,' Molly stirred her tea vigorously, 'had lots of girl friends, but I loved the old rascal for all his faults, and that's what love is all about isn't it? Are you married?' she barked at Abbie.

'Er — no.'

'Keep it that way.' Molly nodded.

'So,' Sim was seated back at the table, all traces of his earlier anger dissipated. 'You've come to do a piece on Diana?'

'The interview will be part of a series on actresses of the seventies. I've several other names lined up but Diana was the only one to confirm.'

'She didn't actually,' Molly broke off from munching a slice of bread.

Two pairs of eyes swivelled in her direction.

'What?' Abbie demanded.

'Don't think she actually knows

anything about you,' Molly didn't look in the least abashed as she confessed, 'forgot to tell her.'

Abbie bit down her dismay at this piece of news. After all her hard work in tracing Diana LaTrobe, it looked as though the project wasn't even going to get off the ground.

'You mean,' Abbie struggled with her words, 'Diana's not expecting me?'

'Not unless she's learned to use a computer in the last few days,' Molly admitted cheerfully. 'I see to all that side of things. Sim does her figures and little Bethan helps out with the cooking.'

'What exactly does Diana do?' Abbie demanded in frustration.

'She's writing a book,' Molly explained, 'or trying to. Don't think it's actually got off the ground yet.'

'A book?' Abbie repeated.

'One of those showbiz memoir affairs. Trouble is,' Molly sniffed, 'she keeps falling out with her researchers and ghost writers.'

'Three at the last count,' Sim nodded agreement.

'Four,' Molly corrected him. She looked hard at Abbie. 'I've got the beginnings of an idea.'

'Oh no,' Sim muttered under his breath.

'Be quiet.' Molly delivered a stern look. 'What I was thinking was,' she took a moment out to sip some more tea, 'would you be interested, Abbie?'

'Interested in what?' she asked.

'With all your journalistic experience you'd be an ideal choice. Don't you think so, Sim?'

'Leave me out of this,' Sim replied.

'I'm sorry?' Abbie frowned. Mentally she had been packing her bag and preparing to say goodbye to Waterside Cottage.

'But I would just say we don't know if Ms Rogers is free, Molly,' Sim put in with a note of caution. 'Not everyone is prepared to fall in with your plans at a moment's notice.'

'Right now you've given me your take

on the matter why don't you butt out?'
Molly turned her spectacles on Sim.

'There's gratitude for you,' Sim
grumbled.

'Shouldn't you be at work?'

'It's Saturday,' Sim pointed out.

'That made no difference in my day.'

'Only because you never had a job,'
Sim began clearing away the breakfast
plates. 'Now I'm going to see if I can
find Bethan. Don't let Molly talk you
into anything you don't want to do, Ms
Rogers,' Sim said.

He left in a swift chill of morning air
as he opened the door and disappeared
into the garden.

'He's a handsome man, isn't he?'
Molly looked after her grandson with a
smile. 'Be a catch for some young lady.
Are you free?'

'Lady LaTrobe,' Abbie began.

'Lady LaTrobe was my mother-in-
law and a woman I loathed. Thought I
wasn't good enough for her son. My
mother thought Justin wasn't good
enough for me.' She tapped Abbie's

hand across the table, 'but never mind all that. I'm speaking out of turn I know, but we've got to get rid of Sim's current girlfriend, she's a disaster. Now if you were interested I could put in a good word for you with Sim?'

Abbie's head was beginning to swim and she began to wish she could join Sim in the garden.

'I thought we were talking about Diana's book.'

'Did I hear my name?'

Looking incredibly beautiful and fresh after only a few hours sleep, Diana swanned into the kitchen wearing a peach silk negligee. Her hair was tied back in a scarf of the same delicate hue.

'Hello, darling,' Molly greeted her daughter. 'Abbie and I were discussing when you and she could make a start on your book.'

'I thought Abbie was a babysitter,' Diana said with a puzzled frown.

'She's a journalist,' Molly brushed aside Diana's comment.

'That's wonderful, darling.' Diana

picked up a piece of Molly's bread and butter. 'I have a window this morning. What say we get together in the library after coffee?'

'Excellent idea.'

Abbie looked from Molly to Diana and back to Molly and knew she was beaten. Perhaps Molly's suggestion might work well, Abbie decided doing a hasty rethink. If she and Diana bonded over their research, she could possibly also get her exclusive interview.

'If you think I'd be suitable, then yes, I accept your offer.'

'You know,' Molly peered hard at Abbie, 'I'm sure I've seen you somewhere before.'

Abbie Is Persuaded To Stay

'Dear old Bubbles,' Diana laughed as yet another photograph slipped out of the leather bound album on to the floor. Diana picked it up. 'The things she used to get up to on set you would not believe. She used to play my younger stepsister in *Masquerade*. She was a girl and a half. I wonder what happened to her.'

The picture was of a mini skirted girl dancing in a fountain, her hair a sodden mess as partygoers squirted her with water from all directions. She was clutching a champagne glass and kicking up her legs in a parody of the Charleston.

'We called her Bubbles because she loved champagne. Her father was something big in the city. 'Spect she's gone all respectable now.' Diana sighed. 'Looking at these photos brings back such memories.'

Abbie looked round helplessly at the growing pile of memorabilia littering the study carpet. There was boxes of programmes, film schedules, pressed flowers, studio publicity posters, letters and masses of photographs.

'Don had a passion for photography,' Diana explained. 'Every new bit of equipment was an absolute must have for him. I can't count the number of times we had to pose for his wretched photo shoots while he tried out the latest technology on me and the boys.'

Diana's generous lips were curved in a smile as she picked up another photo. 'You'd never believe that rather grumpy looking baby glaring at the camera is my Sim, would you? He was normally such a good child but when the mood was on him, if he didn't want to smile, then he wouldn't. Theo was the absolute opposite. Sunny as the day was long was my Theo and such a hit with the other mothers. He always knew how to get his way with women even then. Little devil,' she added indulgently, 'he hasn't changed.'

Diana and Abbie had been sifting through the paperwork for over two hours and as far as Abbie could see they had made absolutely no progress whatsoever. Diana had merely shifted one pile of photographs on to another as she reminisced about the good old days. Her memories were littered with no end of nicknames and spicy stories about her co-stars and some of the parties she had been to. Abbie was beginning to realise why no progress had been made on the proposed book.

'Darling?' Diana looked up from smiling at yet another photo, 'what's wrong?'

'Nothing.' Abbie tried to keep her voice upbeat. It would do no good having a difference of opinion with Diana so early in their relationship.

'Yes there is. You can't fool me. I've seen that face before. It's exactly like the one my old dresser made when she found a tear in one of my costumes and knew she'd be up half the night mending it.' The light laugh hovering on Diana's lips died. 'Actually,' she delved into the nearest pile of photos, 'I'm sure I've got a picture of Orla here somewhere. Where is it now?'

She began searching through the discarded snapshots but without success.

'Haven't you got any sort of filing system?' Abbie asked in exasperation.

Diana pulled a face. 'Not really no, I haven't. I suppose we've got to have one?'

'It would help.'

'I thought you'd say that. Right then, how do we start?' Diana's vivid eyes were fixed hopefully on Abbie. 'Do you have any ideas?'

'Well,' Abbie took a deep breath, 'I've never done this sort of thing before as you know, but I suppose everything needs to be catalogued in chronological order for a start.'

'Good idea. Molly did start putting some stuff on to the computer but I don't think she got very far. Then we had the most dreadful girl come to help me. Darling, she was so dull it was unbelievable. I mean she wore a beige twin-set and pearls for heaven's sake and flat shoes and she had a face that would turn milk sour. It took me all of two weeks to get rid of her and she wasn't the only one.

'The next girl wasn't much better. Nursing a broken heart or some such nonsense. She was always on the telephone to her boyfriend. She left us in the lurch. One morning she just didn't turn up. She'd gone off in the night without a word.'

Abbie could sympathise with her predecessors. She was beginning to suspect that she too had taken on more than she could handle. Her original plan had been to see what she could find out about the diamond brooch she had found amongst her father's possessions, do her interview with Diana then

46

leave, but things weren't going well.

Quite how it had happened she wasn't sure, but somehow she had been inveigled into the Herculean task of making sense of Diana's records on the promise of her requested interview. She had not expected the Foxton family, and she included Molly LaTrobe, to be quite so forceful, charming and persuasive.

Abbie was a total professional when it came to her work and to do a poor job was not her style, even if she had no empathy with the subject. She liked Diana but she sensed the actress would not be of much practical help with the cataloguing.

For the moment she seemed content to sit and go through her mementoes, but for how long? Abbie suspected it only needed Johnny Cavendish to arrive, or one of her friends to suggest an outing and Diana would be off like a shot.

'The laptop's over there,' Diana pointed out helpfully and stretching out her incredibly long legs, she stood up and walked with the practised ease of a trained actress, towards a small table in the corner of the room. 'I haven't a clue how to work it.' She flipped open the lid and stared in hopeless confusion at the blank screen. 'Do you know anything about computers?'

'A little.' Abbie switched it on.

'Darling, how clever you are.' Diana watched as the screen sprang into life. 'There you are then, it's all done, isn't it?'

Abbie did not share Diana's optimism. From the icons on the desktop, she could see Molly had not got very far cataloguing Diana's artefacts. There was a folder marked contacts and another anecdotes and another film appearances.

Abbie clicked the mouse on film appearances. Diana's career had spanned three decades, and although the theatre and television had played a large part in her life, the list of films was also impressive.

'So many memories,' Diana peered

over Abbie's shoulder. 'I remember my leading man in that film,' she pointed to an epic saga about the British Empire. 'He was so short had had to stand on a box to deliver his lines. One day one of the cameramen was fed up with the way the little squirt criticised his lighting, so he hid the thing. The fur ready flew I can tell you, especially when someone suggested he stand on a makeshift vegetable box. We lost a whole day's shooting. He wore a wig too, the leading man, not the cameraman, and that went missing on another occasion. We found it on a garden statue in the grounds of the stately home where we were filming.'

Diana's laughter was so infectious she and Abbie didn't hear the door open behind them.

'I suppose you've forgotten your dental appointment?' Molly enquired from the doorway.

Diana's hand flew to her mouth and she stopped laughing instantly. 'It's not today is it?'

'It was — about five minutes ago. That was the receptionist on the telephone. They've given you another appointment in half an hour's time if you can get to the practice.'

'I must rush.'

'Try not to wind up in a ditch and remember the new speed limit on the road out of Hamwater. You've got enough points for speeding on your licence. You don't want any more,' Molly called after Diana as without a backwards glance at Abbie she fled from the room.

'How are you getting on, petal?' Molly asked.

'We're not,' Abbie admitted.

'I can see you've found my files. Are they any use to you?'

'As far as they go,' Abbie replied diplomatically.

'But they don't go very far, do they?' Molly nodded. 'Diana's got tons of stuff, hasn't she? The publishers have already paid out an advance for the book. They are going to start wanting results soon.' Molly placed her hands on her hips. 'What are you going to do about it?'

'I don't see what I can do,' Abbie admitted. 'You really need good professional help and the work can't be done in a day. It would take at least six weeks and that's a conservative estimate.'

'A suit with a degree in media studies is the last thing we need,' Molly's huge eyes were wide with horror at the thought. 'If you would stay on and help I'd be so grateful,' Molly wheedled, 'I don't want Diana to have to hand back the advance.'

'I'm sure it won't come to that. Diana must still have lots of contacts in the industry. Isn't there someone who would be able to help her from the old days?'

'It's not that.' Molly looked over her shoulder as if to check no one was listening then leaned forward confidentially, 'I've already spent half of it.'

'Half of what?'

'The advance and don't look at me

like that,' Molly retaliated, 'the bike needed an overhaul and I haven't got any money of my own. What was I supposed to do?'

'Not go around spending other people's advances for a start.'

Abbie did her best to sound annoyed with Molly but she couldn't help admiring her for her spirit.

'I'll concede that you've got a point there,' Molly didn't look in the least repentant, 'but let's not argue about all that now. What I need to know is will you help?'

'I've told you I'm not qualified,' Abbie pointed out.

'You're a journalist, aren't you?'

'There's a world of difference between writing an article and doing a book like this. It's a huge project.'

'We don't need you to write it, just sort out the bits and pieces, put names and dates on back of photos, that kind of thing. We'll all help when we've got time.'

Abbie hesitated. She was between

flats ever since her landlord had sold up and moved to France. Now the sale of her parents' bungalow had gone through she was temporarily without a permanent base. A stay of six weeks at Waterside Cottage could prove useful. It would provide her with good copy for her article on actresses in the seventies and at the same time she might be able to discover more about her brooch.

'We'll pay you an advance on your fees.' Sensing Abbie's hesitating Molly pushed for closure. 'We wouldn't want you to work for nothing. How about a down payment now and the rest when you've completed the project? I'll arrange something with Sim this afternoon.'

Abbie's conscience pricked. She was basically an honest person and she had worked her way into the cottage on false pretences. The story about the article was true of course, but that wasn't the only reason she was at Waterside Cottage, and to stay on without mentioning the brooch might be construed as an abuse of Diana's hospitality.

A sly look crept into Molly's eyes. 'Did any other of the actresses you approached answer your request for an interview?'

'No, as a matter of fact they didn't,' Abbie admitted.

'I read your proposal and the actresses you mentioned are notoriously reclusive.'

'That's why I thought it would make a good article.'

'I agree with you and I could give you a personal introduction to three of them.' Molly raised a bushy eyebrow and added, 'if you help us out.'

'That sounds suspiciously like black-mail.'

'Yes, it does, doesn't it?' Molly continued to look unrepentant. 'Whad-dya say? You're a businesswoman, surely you can recognise a good deal when you see one? And what's to lose?'

More than Molly realised, Abbie thought. When she'd found the dia-mond brooch among her father's effects, wrapped in a piece of notepaper headed *Diana LaTrobe* and with the words '*for the baby*' written on it in flamboyant purple ink, Abbie had been convinced interviewing Diana was a good idea, if she wanted to find out about her birth parents. Now she wasn't so sure.

She'd always known she was adopted. Her parents had told her from a very early age that they had chosen her especially and that she was very precious to them. Abbie had been content to leave things at that and until lately she had never experienced the slightest interest in tracing her birth mother or father.

When her mother had died, to be followed six months later by her father who quite simply couldn't live without her, Abbie realised she was alone in the world. That was when she decided to find out something about her true parentage and Molly had extended a tempting bait to persuade Abbie to stay.

'I would need some days off before I start to sort out a few things,' Abbie said playing for time.

'You do that, sweetie,' Molly's lined face softened. She put out a weathered hand and stroked Abbie's auburn hair. 'I'm half Irish too and I've inherited my grandfather's gift of second sight.'

'I'm not Irish,' Abbie began.

'I sense you have another purpose in coming here, besides your interview with Diana. I'm not wrong, am I?' Molly held up a hand. 'It's all right you don't have to answer that one. All I need to know is you're not going to cause any trouble? Diana's got a fair bit of colour in her past. She hasn't exactly been a goody two shoes. I wouldn't want to see my daughter hurt.'

'I'm not interested in any of that,' Abbie said, wondering if she should confide in Molly now.

Before she could speak Molly added, 'I thought not. Then why not take up my offer? You can stay here for a couple of months or so, get Diana's bits and pieces into some sort of shape, do your research, and at the end of the day you'll have three other nice little interviews lined up as well? Deal done?'

Muffled noises and laughter drifted through from the kitchen indicating that Bethan had returned from a horseride.

'Bethan could help you too,' Molly said. 'She's a clever little thing and she knows a lot about the old photographs and I'm sure if Sim's free he'll put in a hand.'

'No,' Abbie snapped.

Molly raised an eyebrow. 'You don't want Sim to help you?'

'It's not that,' Abbie attempted to explain knowing her face was growing red.

'No?'

'Sim doesn't want me here. He suggested I tricked my way into the household by using Bethan as some sort of go between to get my interview with Diana.'

'He can be prickly at times, I'll admit,' Molly said. 'He's so unlike Theo. You would never believe they were brothers.' Molly's brow cleared.

'Now there's an idea. Theo. He's due home shortly. He's filming on some tropical island or other. He would be an ideal helpmate for you. He's always restless and looking for things to do.'

'Molly, will you please stop fixing me up with your grandsons. I have absolutely no interest in either Theo or Sim.'

Again the door had opened quietly behind Abbie. 'I'm pleased to hear it,' she heard Sim's deep voice.

'Sim, there you are.' Molly greeted him. 'Can I have five hundred pounds to give to Abbie please?'

Orla Reflects On Her Past

The deep blue of the Atlantic dazzled Orla Dillaine's green eyes as she leant against the wall in the cobbled harbour, looking out over the bay. Fishing boats bobbed on the water, the swell gently slapping their sides. Seagulls keened and swooped overhead, always on the lookout for titbits left by the tourists.

She raised her face to the early morning sunshine. It was bright and sharp. She loved this time of year, when everything was fresh and young and smelt newly washed and ready for action. The harbour was waking up after the slower winter months and soon the quay would be full of pleasure craft and visitors, providing a much needed injection of cash into the local community.

Some of the cafés were already putting out their summer chairs and tables under the awnings hoping to attract some early custom. If Orla didn't have such a hectic schedule she might have been tempted to linger for a coffee and pastry at Ma's. She provided the best homemade patisserie for miles around and her Porter cake was to die for.

Busy as Orla was, these days her life was far removed from the dizzy time she'd spent in the world of showbiz. She didn't miss her old life at all but mornings like this brought back memories of the heady days when she had been at the centre of things. She had been young and life had been exciting and full and lived at a frantic pace.

In her middle fifties she wasn't old now, but these days she preferred the gentler pace of working in her studio, crafting her pieces of Celtic jewellery and selling them to the tourists who visited her harbour workshop on their way to Cork to kiss the Blarney Stone.

She took a deep breath of fresh morning air. It was full of the smells of roaring surf and sandy beach and the lobster catch being unloaded from one of the fishing boats. Thunderclouds were gathering on the horizon but Orla knew it was only a spring storm. It would be swift and soon pass over and the rain would be soft and cleansing.

'Mornin', Orla.' One of the farm-hands greeted her as he made his way up the hill on his way to work.

She waved back then turned slowly. It was going to be a full day. A busload of tourists was booked in for her course on the history of jewellery making and the ancient designs she used as the basis for her work.

Orla liked to provide a little local colour to her courses and her lectures were peppered with stories about Irish folklore and the history of the area.

There was lunch to organise too — soup and poached salmon in the usual seafood restaurant she patronised followed by a display of Irish singing and dancing, then a stroll round the harbour for everyone to walk off all their excesses before her guests boarded their bus for their next destination.

Orla liked to give full value to her customers and the number of personal recommendations she received was a measure of her success. She'd recently branched out into online jewellery sales and early orders were promising.

Ever since the death of her beloved father last winter, she had liked to keep herself busy. It was the first time in her life that she had lived alone and she sometimes found during the quiet evenings her thoughts would dwell on the past and there were parts of her past it was painful to remember.

With brisk strides she made her way back to her studio. Dreaming about the old days and mooning around the harbour was not the way to get things done. She had a busy day ahead of her. It was time to get things moving.

Her studio was a modern open plan building, built on two levels with large windows designed to catch the best of the morning sunshine. Everything was state of the art and no expense had been spared. If there was one thing Orla had learned from Diana LaTrobe it was never to do things by halves.

'Don't go for the cheapest. You'll only regret not going for the best later,' had been the best advice she had given Orla.

Financing the studio had cost almost every penny Orla had in the world, but her profits were already up on last year, and next year Orla was hoping to get permission to build another extension.

Her generous mouth curved into a smile. From where she'd inherited her business acumen she had no idea. Her father had been a simple farmhand and although her brothers had moved to the city, they were only office employees.

Perhaps it had been Diana's influence. She was an extremely savvy lady who worked hard and expected those around her to do the same. How Diana had driven Orla mad, and how she'd so loved working for her. No two days had ever been the same. Life had been a constant round of schedules, deadlines, parties, work, more parties and awards.

The demands on Diana's wardrobe had been unceasing and many was the night Orla had worked through until the small hours until her fingers ached and she'd almost fallen asleep at her machine, making sure every button and every loose thread was secured and up to the punishing workout it would receive the moment it was needed on set.

Diana was a charmer to work for, but she demanded a high standard of work — get her on a bad day and, as Orla could testify from experience, the fur would fly if things weren't up to scratch.

When they'd been filming *Masquerade*, the pressure had been so intense, Orla required assistants of her own to keep up with the demand for the designer wardrobe Diana had needed for her role of Lady Alexandra, matriarch of the aristocratic family who was the centre of the soap opera that had the nation riveted to their television sets twice a week.

Sometimes the goings on on the film sets rivalled those of the make believe work of *Masquerade*. It had been an unreal life and Orla was glad to have been part of it at the time.

It was during rare lulls in the filming schedules that she had discovered her talent for designing jewellery. The paste examples of Lady Alexandra's collection had excited her interest and some of her sketches had even been commissioned for use in the series itself. Orla's father had been so proud of her for that one, and she was pleased he had been given the chance to boast to his friends about his daughter's prowess.

Dismissing thoughts of her past life, Orla ran a swift eye over the arrangements made for the day's course. Everything was laid out and ready for her students. Orla's work experience team had seen to that. She liked to help youngsters who were on the point of leaving school and made it a point of using local help to set up her workshops. It provided them with a feel for the discipline and responsibility they would need for whatever career path they chose in the future.

She glanced at the mounted wall clock. There was still another half an hour to go before she could expect the first of her arrivals. There was just time to catch up on some paperwork. She strolled over to her computer and checked her email inbox.

The name, Johnny Cavendish, flashed up in the messages received folder. With a smile of pleasure Orla clicked on his message.

Hi, Orla, darling, she read, how are you?

The corners of Orla's eyes softened. Johnny could charm the birds off the trees and had a reputation with the ladies. At one time they had been very close not in a romantic sense, but as true friends and they had remained friends over the years. Johnny had stuck by Orla and helped her when her life was in turmoil and for that she would always be grateful.

A little bit of news you may find interesting, his message continued, *Dee's been commissioned to write a book about the old days. Well, you know her, she's been writing it on and off for years, but this time it's serious. There's been a resurgence of interest in Masquerade since one of the satellite television channels has been showing repeats of the old episodes. Dee's been doing interviews and day time chat shows and loving every minute of it. She's had an advance from a publisher for her book proposal. Trouble is Molly's gone and spent it on that wretched bike of hers.*

Orla laughed out loud as she read Johnny's email. Lady Molly was another one she'd got on well with, another true friend. The two of them had spent many nights on her little houseboat dishing the dirt while they enjoyed a nightcap. Their sessions often developed into impromptu parties when Diana's guests drifted down from Waterside Cottage for a breath of evening air by the river and to see what the noise was all about.

Anyway, Orla read on, *Dee's got herself some professional help in the form of a young journalist who turned up here the other night. Turned out Molly had arranged an interview and forgot to tell Dee anything about it. Typical. The girl's name is Abbie Rogers and she's agreed to stay on and help out. Hope she'll be able to lick Dee's records into some sort of shape.*

Funny thing is the moment I saw the girl I was reminded of you. She's got your lovely hair and eyes. That's when I realised I hadn't been in touch with you for ages. If I can't get over to the old Emerald Isle for a chinwag about the old days and a bit of golf, you must come and visit. Be good to catch up? What do you say? Keep me up to speed with all your news. Lots of love, Johnny.

A sound in the courtyard outside drew Orla's attention away from the computer. A bus and a four track had driven in. Her students had arrived and were already spilling out of their coach. The work experience trainees were forming a welcome committee and the courtyard was a hubbub of noise and laughter as old friends recognised each other.

Orla switched the computer on to screen save. There would be time to think about Johnny's news later. Right now she had work to do.

She walked outside to greet the new arrivals, firmly dismissing from her mind all thoughts of young female journalists with auburn hair.

Abbie Meets Theo Foxton

Had she done the right thing? Abbie bit her lip as she turned off the main road. It had been a wrench finally leaving Devon. She had lived there on and off nearly all her life. Even after college and her move to London Abbie had visited her parents whenever she could. As rural Dorset gave way to the palm fringed Devon coastline and she caught her first glimpse of the sea her blood would always quicken from the joy of being home.

Her father had retired from the church only three years before his death and he and Abbie's mother had bought a small holiday bungalow by the sea. They'd soon integrated themselves into the local community and Abbie loved sharing her rare days off with them.

They never did anything special, just a little gardening, or a walk along the seafront ending up with a meal in a local restaurant. Her mother enjoyed her line dancing classes in the parish hall as a way of keeping fit and Abbie always joined in whenever she visited.

Abbie squinted in the late morning sunshine and lowered her sun visor to keep out the glare from the windscreen. She was at a crossroads in her life and it would do no good looking back. This job with Diana would tide her over until she decided what to do next with her life.

She enjoyed the variety of her job as a freelance journalist revelling in the excitement of each new assignment. Molly had promised her several introductions so the future was looking bright.

Abbie turned up the radio and sang along with the music, her natural optimism kicking in. There was a lot to look forward to. She'd always loved the water and Molly had also promised to treat her to a picnic on her houseboat one day when the weather was fine and when they had some spare time.

'I'm always down there,' she confided to Abbie as they sat at the kitchen table while Abbie absolutely insisted they made out a written contract for the proposed work in hand. 'I have to get away every now and then. I love my daughter to bits, but it's not unknown for us to rub each other up the wrong way.'

There was a bump from the back of the car as one of Abbie's bags slipped off the seat and on to the floor. Abbie slowed down fractionally not wanting further disruption of her load.

Diana hadn't raised the least objection when Abbie explained that as she was between flats she would need to bring most of her belongings with her while she was cataloguing Diana's memorabilia.

'One thing we are not short of, darling, is space.' Diana had waved an expansive hand. 'There's plenty of room to store your bits and pieces. Bring whatever you like. It will be lovely to have someone young about the place. Molly can be very difficult at times.'

That last comment had provoked a frank exchange of views between Diana and Molly, which had left Abbie reeling, but a few moments later the pair of them were laughing together and exchanging jokes as if nothing had happened.

The sun was warm through the car window and Abbie wound it down taking a deep breath of spring air. Spring, it was her favourite time of the year, the season of new beginnings. She inhaled the smells of damp earth mingled with primroses.

The sign to Hamwater came up and Abbie turned quickly down the minor road that led to Waterside Cottage. There were no paint markings in the middle of the road and Abbie stopped her singing to concentrate. She had already passed two horse riders earlier on and needed to take care, there were very few passing places and with her heavy load she had no wish to have an accident.

A dark shape suddenly loomed at her from out of the trees. Stifling a shriek Abbie swerved to avoid it. The car jolted and came to halt at a slew in the middle of the road. Breathing heavily, she took a few moments out to recover herself.

'What on earth do you think you're playing at?' she demanded when she realised the shape was actually a human being looking as startled as she was. 'I nearly went into the ditch.' She finished her tirade with a gasped, 'You.'

She found herself looking into the apologetic golden brown eyes of Sim Foxton. He was dressed in a business suit and carrying a briefcase and couldn't have looked more out of place down a country lane.

'I'm sorry,' he apologised. 'My fault entirely. I wasn't paying attention. We don't get much traffic down this road. Er — how are you?'

'Fine,' Abbie snapped back, 'no thanks to you.'

Again Abbie wished she had paid

more attention to her hair and wasn't dressed in a rather ancient tank top and an old skirt she used to wear to sunbathe in the garden of her parents' bungalow. Most of her good clothes were packed in her bags and she hadn't wanted to unpack them before leaving her friend's house early that morning, so she had grabbed the first available set of clothes she could find. She was now more than ever aware of her dishevelled appearance.

'You're back,' Sim said.

He smiled and if Abbie hadn't known better she would have thought he was pleased to see her. His eyes softened at the corners. Abbie frowned. They weren't in the least bit like Diana's. Her eyes were greeny blue and almond shaped, almost feline and there was no way Sim had inherited her elegant bone structure. His build was of the solid farmer's stock variety.

'So it would seem,' Abbie replied to Sim's remark tucking a stray tendril of hair behind her ear. She could feel her topknot slipping and feared her scrunchie might give way at any moment. It was always the same when her hair was freshly washed. Before she'd set out that morning there hadn't been time to dry it properly after her shower. There hadn't been time for anything much over the past few months.

After clearing out her parents' bungalow and house sitting a friend's flat while she was away on holiday, she had then had to make arrangements to move some of her things into storage. Her head was in a whirl and drying her hair and wearing new clothes were low on her current list of priorities.

'Er, you don't look dressed for a country walk.' Abbie's eyes rested on the briefcase Sim was holding.

He gave an embarrassed smile. 'I don't, do I? I've been up at the golf club sorting out one or two things. I thought I'd better look the part. The committee are a bit old fashioned when it comes to business meetings and insist on the wearing of ties. They can also be a bit pompous at times and I think I put one or two noses out of joint when I suggested streamlining their accounts system. Things got a bit heated. That's why I wasn't looking where I was going. I needed a walk to clear my head.

'The Captain offered me a lift as I haven't got my car today but he wasn't going all the way to Hamwater so I said I'd walk the rest. I took the short cut.' Sim looked ruefully down at his shoes and admitted with a wry smile, 'I wish I hadn't now. We had a lot of rain a couple of weeks ago. I'd forgotten how muddy it was.' He scraped the mess off his shoes on a patch of damp grass then looked expectantly at Abbie.

'If you don't mind sharing the front seat with a suitcase I can give you a lift,' she offered.

It was the last thing she wanted to do but in the circumstances Abbie could hardly refuse.

'I'll try not to make a mess,' he promised, eyeing up her luggage. 'On the way to a jumble sale are you?'

Abbie reversed her car back into a straight line. The temptation to run over Sim's muddy shoes was almost too much for her. Just when she was beginning to like him, he came out with a remark like that. Not trusting herself to speak she leaned across and opened the passenger door.

Sim eased his long legs into the seat beside Abbie. She heard him groan as he banged his knees on the dashboard.

'Sorry,' she said, hiding a triumphant little smile. 'I had to put the seat forward,' she explained, 'to get all my jumble in the back.'

'Exactly how long are you moving in for?' Sim enquired. He would have looked round to inspect the mountain of luggage but his vision was obscured by a painting wedged behind his seat.

'I made arrangements with Diana,' Abbie clipped back at him, 'to store some of my things at Waterside Cottage. I'm between flats,' she explained, 'but you needn't worry I'm not taking up permanent residence at the cottage.'

'Pleased to hear it.' Abbie ignored the amusement in Sim's voice. 'I mean I know we've got a lot of room, but there are limits.'

Abbie gripped the steering wheel, determined not to rise to the bait.

'Look, I know you don't want me at Waterside Cottage, but Diana does and as she is paying me a very generous fee for the job in hand and what you think of the arrangement is really none of your business, so will you do me a favour and butt out?'

'I see you possess all the temperament of a person with reddish hair.'

'Your attitude would drive anyone over the top, no matter what colour hair they had.'

'Sorry.' Sim's apology took Abbie by surprise. 'You're quite right. I was out of order. What Diana does is her own affair. Shall we start again? I had a bad morning with the committee at the Golf Club and I had no right to take my frustration out on you.'

Abbie wished Sim would continue

being unpleasant. She didn't know how to deal with a Sim who apologised and admitted he was in the wrong.

'Is this a painting of somewhere you know?' Sim asked after a few moments of silence. He inspected the picture wedged behind him.

'It was my parents' bungalow in Devon. A friend gave it to them as a housewarming gift.'

'You're from Devon? Thought I recognised the burr,' he said. 'Were you born in the West Country?'

Abbie hated talking about herself and didn't welcome people prying into her private life. Her parents had told her as much about her past as they knew but it distressed her mother when Abbie asked questions, so in the end she stopped asking. As the years passed she began to think of them as her real parents and it was only on her father's death so soon after her mother's that Abbie recalled the circumstances of her birth.

The discovery of the brooch in

Diana's headed notepaper amongst his things had been the spur to her contacting the actress, and she would do well to remember that, she reminded herself sternly before she became too involved with likes of Sim Foxton.

'I was born in London,' she admitted.

'So was I,' Sim said. 'What part?'

'I really don't know,' Abbie replied truthfully. 'I moved to Devon as a baby and that was the only home I knew.'

'Sounds lovely,' Sim replied with a trace of envy in his voice.

Abbie looked at him in surprise.

'For most of my childhood we lived in a draughty old vicarage that always smelt of soot and damp and there was never any money for luxuries.'

The discomfort and lack of material possessions hadn't made the slightest bit of difference to Abbie. The vicarage was always full of laughter and love and the important things in life.

'I suspect life with Diana was a lot more glamorous and comfortable.'

'Being the son of the famous Diana LaTrobe wasn't exactly easy for me or Theo,' Sim replied.

Abbie cast him a disbelieving look. 'Bet you never took turns in the bath because there was only enough hot water for one.'

'Maybe not,' Sim delivered a devilish smile in her direction, 'but I wouldn't have minded.

'Theo and I tried to keep out of the spotlight but if Diana wasn't in the headlines, Molly was usually up to something. They were always in the newspaper. That sort of thing can be pretty embarrassing when you're growing up.'

'I can imagine.'

'Can you?' Sim didn't look convinced.

Abbie experienced an unexpected pang of sympathy for him.

'Sort of. I know my embarrassment isn't in the same league as yours, but every year my father would insist on taking part in the father's race on school sports day. He always came last and he had a peculiar way of running which involved using both his arms as well as his legs. He looked really silly. I felt honour bound to stand on the touchline cheering him on but I knew all my classmates sniggered behind my back. I tried to persuade him not to take part but he said it was a tradition and if it made people happy to see him make a fool of himself then he was quite happy to keep up the tradition.'

'Your father sounds quite a philosopher,' Sim said.

'He was a lovely man,' Abbie said. Looking at the road ahead and blinking to clear her blurred vision, she missed the softening of the expression in Sim's eyes.

'Your father was Don Foxton wasn't he?' Abbie asked changing the subject.

Her research had revealed Don and Diana Foxton had been the showbiz royalty of the day, and no party was complete without their presence.

'The impresario? Yes. He died when I

was seven. Theo was five.'

'And Diana married again?'

'Yes. Barney was a cameraman,' Sim said carefully. 'He died too.'

Abbie sensed there was more, but when Sim didn't elaborate she said, 'Your background's been a lot more colourful than mine.'

Sim flashed Abbie his brief smile. 'I'm glad you've come to stay,' he said as they turned into the driveway of Waterside Cottage.

'You are?' Abbie raised her eyebrows.

'We need someone rational about the place. Diana's totally scatty and as for Molly and her wretched motorbike crowd, you don't want to know about them.'

'There's Bethan,' Abbie said. 'She seems a very happy child.' As they drove up to the front door of Waterside Cottage it was flung open and the next moment the forecourt was full of barking dogs, an excited child, a marmalade cat and Johnny Cavendish.

'Abbie,' Bethan shrieked, 'you were gone so long I thought you weren't

84

coming back. Uncle Sim said . . . '

'Never mind all that,' Johnny butted in. 'Good to see you, Abbie,' Johnny opened the door courteously and helped her out, delivering a smacking kiss on her cheek. 'You couldn't have come at a better time. Molly and Diana aren't speaking and Molly's ridden off in a huff on that bike of hers. Diana's retreated to her room with a migraine and to cap it all,' Johnny paused for dramatic effect, 'Theo's . . . '

'There's more?' Sim demanded bending down to hug his niece.

'Daddy's home.' Bethan was jumping up and down in excitement. 'And he says he's going to help Abbie with her research. You'll love Daddy, Abbie, he's the most beautiful man in the world.'

Abbie glanced across to Sim who stiffened as he looked up. Abbie followed the direction of his eyes.

Standing in the doorway to Waterside Cottage was a tall thin man who was the closest thing Abbie had ever seen to a modern day cavalier. His hair was unkempt, dark and curly and the expression in his eyes suggested he knew exactly what Abbie was thinking.

'How do you do?' He walked towards Abbie very slowly and extended his hand. 'I'm Theo Foxton,' he glanced across at Sim. 'I'm Sim's younger brother, Bethan's father.'

Abbie looked from Theo to Sim. She didn't think she had ever seen two brothers who were so unlike each other. Sim with his stocky build, dark brown hair and hazel eyes was a stark contrast to the piercing blue eyes and jet black hair of his brother.

'I'm sure we're going to be the best of friends,' Theo squeezed Abbie's fingers. 'Now come inside before the wind disturbs that glorious top knot of golden hair, otherwise I might just be persuaded to readjust it for you and that would never do, would it?'

Without a word, Sim turned on his heel and strode into the house. Theo watched him go with a taunting look in his eyes.

'She's The Daughter
I Always Wanted'

It had been a long and riotous lunch. Johnny's culinary skills extended to a creditable coq au vin. 'Dish I learned to cook when I lived in Provence for six months and had a French lady friend.' He twirled an imaginary moustache.

He smiled towards Diana who was in her element, seated at the top of the table looking absolutely stunning in a figure hugging silk dress that should have been outrageous on a female of her years.

'I so love having all my family here,' Diana announced, her migraine having miraculously disappeared at the sound of the excited voices downstairs. 'My two boys, my lovely Bethan, my darling Johnny and my daughter, Abbie.'

Abbie choked on a slice of Johnny's

tarte aux pommes, another dish he informed her he had picked up on a stay in France.

'Abbie's not your daughter, Diana,' Bethan squealed with laughter as Abbie coughed and hid her face in her paper napkin, to hide her heightened colour.

'She's the daughter I always wanted,' Diana said in a soft voice. Her eyes would have melted the hardest heart as she asked Abbie, 'You don't mind, do you?'

'Mind what?' Abbie asked, clearing her throat in confusion and fighting off the beginnings of a headache.

Unlike many of her contemporaries she did not like drinking at lunchtime and had only indulged in a few mouthfuls of wine when Theo had tempted her to have a glass as a toast to welcome him home.

'Being my honorary daughter while you're here?'

'For heaven's sake, Diana, you're embarrassing Abbie,' Sim cut in with an angry frown.

'Good old Sim, always the party pooper. Nothing changes,' Theo replied leaning back in his chair and stretching out his long legs, the expression in his eyes confrontational.

Antagonism bristled between the two brothers as Sim glared back at his brother.

'It's always like this,' Johnny said in a lowered voice to Abbie. He leaned his head towards her so that only she could hear him say, 'Ever since Theo ran off and married Sim's fiancée.'

Her gasp of surprise was cut short by Bethan saying, 'I know something you don't know, Diana. Abbie's real mother gave her a beautiful brooch. She showed it to me.'

'A brooch?' Diana asked into the silence that had fallen around the table. 'What sort of brooch?'

'It's got diamonds in it,' Bethan announced importantly, aware that she was now the centre of attention. 'We were looking at it in the study, the night Abbie arrived, weren't we?'

'Could I see this brooch?' Diana asked with a pleasant smile. 'I'm quite a connoisseur when it comes to jewellery.'

'I'm not sure where it is,' Abbie replied wishing everyone wasn't looking at her quite so intently. It had been a mistake showing it to Bethan she realised now, but it was too late to do anything about it.

'Not surprised,' Sim came to her aid with, 'have you seen what your protégée's got in her car, Diana? Half of Devon by the look of things, goodness knows where we're going to put it all.'

'Devon?' drawled Theo, 'where does Devon come into all this?'

'I used to live there with my parents.'

'Don't think I've ever been to Devon,' Theo said. 'Have you Diana?'

'Your father and I once stayed in the sweetest little bed and breakfast farmhouse with Orla and Barney. We were filming on location and had the weekend off when one of the cameramen became ill. Half the wardrobe staff went down with the bug too. Rather than soldier on, they gave us all forty-eight hours leave with instructions to get well. Don and I had a lovely time. It was like a second honeymoon. Yes, I've fond memories of Devon. What part do you come from, Abbie?'

'In a small village outside Budleigh Salterton.'

Abbie jumped as Sim put his hand over hers on the table.

His flesh felt warm to the touch. She turned enquiring eyes in his direction.

'I felt like doing that,' he said with disarming frankness, 'we're a very tactile family and you looked a bit sad.'

'Quite right, Sim,' Theo enthused, 'I'd have done it myself but that would have meant crawling all over Johnny to get to Abbie and I don't think Diana would have taken too kindly to that sort of behaviour at the dinner table. Can I be second in line after you've finished stroking her hand?'

Abbie laughed reluctantly. The whole family was outrageous, but she sensed under their glamour they were kind hearted, if a tad unconventional. She looked across to where Diana was smiling at her still unable to fathom out why her father should be in possession of her brooch — if it was hers.

Was there a connection between herself and Diana? They didn't look alike.

Diana was tall and tanned, unbelievably chic, beautiful, fringe aristocracy, whereas Abbie had hair the colour of Pippin apples and a complexion that could only take half an hour's sun at the most before it turned pink and her eyes puffed up.

'You've grown into a beautiful woman,' Diana said so softly, Abbie thought she had imagined it. No one else gave any indication that they had overheard her words.

'What I really need,' Johnny boomed, clapping his hands for silence and creating a welcome interruption, 'is a family photo.'

'Not more photos,' Theo complained, 'haven't we got enough of the things to

92

go through already?'

'We haven't got one of Abbie. Come on,' Johnny coaxed her, 'flash those lovely eyes at the camera for me and say cheese.' Before she could protest he clicked his camera at her. 'Another one, because you blinked,' he insisted.

'I don't think you got me in it at all,' Theo complained, 'I think you were only aiming your lens at Abbie. What do you want her photo for anyway? Not thinking of putting it up on Diana's website as her long lost daughter are you? Now that would make headlines.'

'Sometimes you say the stupidest things, Theo,' Sim snapped an angry frown creasing his brow.

'It was only a joke,' Theo insisted.

Abbie squirmed in her seat. She didn't like the way Diana was looking at her, or Theo come to that. Sim wasn't looking exactly friendly either.

Johnny replaced his camera in its case and glanced at his watch. 'We really should be getting a move on, Dee. It's nearly three o'clock. You hadn't forgotten we're due in town this evening?'

'Do we have to go?' Diana objected. 'I'd far rather stay here with the young people and go through some of those photos.'

'You've been saying that for months and you never do go through them, so yes we do have to go out.'

'And I have to get back to my office,' Sim said. 'Can you give me a lift, Johnny?'

'My pleasure,' he replied. 'Come on, Dee, move yourself. Bye, Abbie,' he kissed her on the cheek, the pad of his thumb rough against her skin. 'You know I really am glad you found us.'

'Found you?' Abbie frowned at him.

'That night we mistook you for the babysitter?' He squeezed her hand. 'You could have so easily driven off into the night like the real babysitter and we would never have met you.'

'Johnny,' she lowered her voice and leaned in towards him, 'do you . . . ' she began.

'Sorry, can't stop now. If I don't get Dee out of the house in the next five minutes we'll never make London in time.'

'I'm going to take the dogs for a walk,' Bethan announced, 'down to the stables. Paddy's got a sore fetlock and I can't ride him until the vet has a look at it.'

'That leaves you and me,' Theo said as everyone vacated the kitchen and he and Abbie were alone. 'What say we make a start on Diana's photos?' he asked. 'I think I can help you. We had to do something similar after one of my trips to the rainforests of the Amazon. Someone messed up the sequence of shots and we had to start all over again. Once you get stuck in, it's not so difficult.'

'Of course, you're *the* Theo Foxton.' Abbie looked at him in recognition. 'How could I not have realised earlier? I love your wildlife programmes on the television. My father never missed an episode if he could possibly help it. We used to have to record them if he was out.'

Theo looked inordinately pleased and surprisingly rather embarrassed by the enthusiasm of Abbie's praise. 'He did? That's wonderful. You've no idea how gruelling it can be in some of these places, working for hours on end just to get a few seconds of film in the can.

'Then you start to wonder if anybody is actually going to watch the programme and if it's ever going to get made. I mean I think I've got the most marvellous job in the world but I can't help feeling one day I'm going to be sussed and the bubble will burst and people will realise I'm a fraud and then I'll have to go back to sweeping the streets or something equally horrendous.'

'That's ridiculous. You won that award didn't you?'

Theo gave a modest shrug of his shoulders. 'I didn't win it. It was a team effort and I accepted it on their behalf.

I'd be nowhere without the rest of the crew.'

'Well I think you're wonderful.'

Theo's embarrassment deepened. 'Really?' He cleared his throat to cover his confusion. 'Diana tells me you're a journalist. Have I read anything of yours?'

'My stuff is much more low key,' Abbie admitted. 'I did an in depth piece on a deposed South American dictator but it never saw the light of day because most editors felt the subject matter was too hot to handle.'

'It's a pity when that sort of thing happens, isn't it? But I'm sure you'll get your big break. Keep pegging away and one day it will all fall into place. Listen to your Uncle Theo, he knows about these things.'

'I wouldn't have got this job if Molly hadn't rigged it for me,' Abbie admitted.

A shadow crossed Theo's face. 'Our Molly's usually up to every trick in the book. You wouldn't believe what she and that husband of hers got up to in their day.'

'I think I might,' Abbie was forced to admit.

'Of course Sim's her blue-eyed boy,' Theo said with a petulant twist to his mouth.

'Do you think Molly's all right?' Abbie asked, not wanting to get involved in family politics.

'What do you mean?'

'Going off on her motorbike like that after an argument with Diana?'

'She'll be fine. She's probably only gone over to her houseboat. It's her bolthole on the canal. It's a nice little houseboat. Remind me to take you over there one day. Come on,' he grabbed Abbie's hand. 'Let's go into the study and attack that pile of photographs.'

They surveyed the piles of papers and photos that someone had attempted to put in some sort of order.

'I don't know if I'm up to this,' Abbie confessed, 'paperwork's not really one of my strengths.'

'That's not the sort of talk we want to hear, Ms Rogers.' Theo pretended to frown at her. 'Now why don't we start on the *Masquerade* photos first?' he suggested. 'How about if I can tell you who everyone is and you can write it on the back? I know if I was ghost writing Diana's memoirs I'd be eternally grateful for information of that nature.'

'Do you know who everyone is?' Abbie asked.

'Course I do,' Theo assured her, 'and if I don't recognise them I'll invent a name. Fancy some music to get us in the mood?' Theo's full lips curled into a seductive smile. 'If things get too tedious we can always lighten up with a turn or two about the floor.'

He slotted a disc into the player and the next moment the room was filled with the strains of a Mozart concerto.

'There, that's better, isn't it? You know,' Theo squatted down on the floor beside Abbie, 'you really do have the most amazing colour hair.' He put a hand out and stroked it. 'You remind me of a Celtic princess — or a mermaid.'

Abbie shifted away from him. Theo was too dangerously attractive for comfort. His deep laugh made her fingertips tingle.

'Sorry, I shouldn't tease you, should I?'

'Shall we start on this pile?' Abbie asked, picking up the top album of photos.

'Yes, miss,' Theo said with a sigh.

* * *

It was difficult not to respond to his easygoing charm and Abbie feared it might not have been a good idea to involve him in the project, but contrary to her doubts, he proved an efficient and informative assistant, able to identify everyone in the numerous photos she thrust before him.

'I used to do this for Barney, my stepfather,' he explained. 'I had a whole term off school once after a skiing accident. I was bed-bound and going quietly up the wall and making everyone's life hell, so Barney made me write up his photos of Diana. That's my schoolboy scrawl on the back of this one. Look.' He turned it over. 'It was taken on the set of *Masquerade*. There's Diana and her leading man, can't remember his name and there's Johnny in the background. He was always hanging around even in those days.

'He often appeared as an extra. He wore a white dinner jacket well and was always good as the ex-pat.'

Theo's blue eyes lit up as he recognised another face. 'And there's Orla. I don't really remember much about her, but Barney told me she was Diana's dresser.' Theo frowned. 'I wonder what happened to her. There was a rumour about her and my father, not that I knew anything about it. I was far too young.'

'What sort of rumour?' Abbie asked.

'Dad had a bit of an eye for the

ladies. I think that's why Diana and Orla parted company. My real father and Orla were getting too close. I was only a toddler at the time.'

'Telling tales out of school?' Molly's crisp voice broke in.

'Someone's got to look after Abbie,' Theo greeted his grandmother. 'Everyone's deserted us.'

Abbie scrambled to her feet. 'We were making a start on the cataloguing,' she began.

'Give me a kiss.' Molly held out her arms, her leathery face full of smiles. 'I thought you weren't coming back.' Her white hair was soft against Abbie's cheek. 'You naughty girl. Diana and I had this fearful row about you. I told her she was wrong.'

The wiry little body against hers felt strangely comforting, like being cuddled by a loving grandmother.

Abbie smiled. 'Didn't you believe I was as good as my word?'

'I did,' Molly insisted, 'but Sim had already told me not to expect to see you against after we'd given you that advance. I blew a gasket when Diana started on about it too this morning.'

'Sim said what?' Abbie screwed up her face in disbelief.

'Nothing,' Molly muttered and hung her head.

'Diana told me,' Theo interrupted, 'that Sim said you wouldn't come back because Molly had given you too much money and you were probably on your way to Acapulco on the proceeds of having worked a flanker on us.'

Abbie didn't think she had ever been so annoyed.

'That's outrageous. What right has he got to say things like that about me when he hardly knows me?'

'That's our Sim, I'm afraid. Doesn't trust any female after his fiancée ran off with another man.'

'Correct me if I'm wrong, Theo,' Abbie said in a voice that would have sliced a glacier, 'but didn't she run off with you?'

As the full impact of her words sunk in, the only sound in the room was that of Molly cackling loudly in the background.

'It's Too Much Of A Coincidence'

'As I live and breathe, Johnny Cavendish.' Orla gaped at the man standing in the forecourt of her studio, then a smile of pleasure lit up her face. He was older, his hair was silver streaked now and he had put on a few pounds, but there was no disguising the roguish smile and the slightly rakish air. He held out his arms and she ran towards him. The next moment she was enfolded in a bear hug that took her breath away.

'You still smell of those peppermints you were always sucking,' she murmured into his tweed jacket.

'Aids the digestion. Want one?' h fumbled in his pocket and produced tube of sweets. 'Nothing like a peppe mint for celebrating a reunion of lo lost friends.'

'What are you doing here?' Orla demanded when she eventually managed to break free and after she had popped one of Johnny's mints into her mouth.

'Do I have to have a reason to visit my beautiful Irish colleen?' he protested.

'I should say you do,' she retorted. 'It must be over twenty years since I last saw you.'

'Dear girl, for heaven's sake,' he looked over his shoulder then lowered his voice, 'my reputation will be in tatters if you go round telling everyone how old I am. I don't admit to being a day over fifty and I'd thank you to remember that.'

'Neither of us is as young as we used to be,' Orla chided him, 'you old fraud, and if I've got older then so have you.'

'Some women will always be young and beautiful, Orla and you're one of them. Let me take a good look at you. That's a stunning outfit you're wearing. Do you still make your own things?'

'I do.'

Orla did a twirl. These days her shining mane of auburn hair was more tamed than Johnny remembered, but the eyes were the same mystical shade of green.

'Hah,' he smiled, 'you've still got that golden dusting of freckles across the bridge of your nose.'

'Too much time spent out on the water,' Orla admitted.

'In that little boat, the one you were always telling us about?'

'The currach? The very same.' Orla laughed. 'If I'm not fishing, I'm sketching. But what are we doing standing about outside? Come in.'

Johnny followed Orla's elegant figure through the main reception hall and up the stairs to the tiny kitchen she kept for her own personal purposes.

'Tea?'

'Please. I must say it's a lovely set up you've got here,' Johnny said admiring the view over the harbour.

'It's been a struggle, but business is

really taking off at last,' Orla's face was full of enthusiasm. 'I've several courses fully booked over the next few months and I've a deal going with a local restaurant. They provide fresh catering for my students at a friendly price. We do music evenings and there's always a dance every weekend.'

'Sounds magical. Where is everyone today?' Johnny asked looking down at the forecourt. 'The place is deserted.'

'I'm in between courses. I like time to myself to catch up. There's coursework to prepare and I've got to update my jewellery stock on the website, then there's the paperwork to see to. I hardly have a moment to spare.'

'I'm impressed.' Johnny took the mug of tea Orla offered him. 'You never used to be so business-like in the old days.'

'Let's sit on the balcony,' Orla said. 'We can catch the best of the afternoon sun.'

'You know a man could fall in love with this place,' Johnny said as he settled down in a canvas-backed chair and watched the comings and goings on the harbour front. A catch was being unloaded and the air was redolent with the tang of sea salt.

'Whenever I have to go away I miss it so much,' Orla replied. 'Everywhere is so green and fresh and I have to live by the sea. I was born here and the sea is in my bones.'

'Do you live in the studio?'

'Sometimes, but I've a cottage nearby if I need to get away. I like to go organic every so often.'

'And you live alone?'

Orla nodded. 'Never married, foot-loose and fancy free, that's me.'

'You don't miss the old days?' Johnny asked softly.

Orla sipped some tea before saying, 'Occasionally, but it seems like another world now, a bit of a dream.' There was sadness in her smile as she asked, 'How is Diana?'

'The same as usual, full of life, creating havoc, still arguing with Molly.'

'I've been watching the re-runs of

Masquerade on television. She was so beautiful.'

'She still is.'

'I'm sure. No one could ever believe . . . ' Orla shook her head and didn't finish what she was saying.

'Believe what?' Johnny queried.

'I wish we'd parted friends,' Orla replied.

'You mean that business with her husband?'

'There was no business as such, but I don't think Diana ever believed me.'

'You were young and very beautiful, Don was charismatic and oozed charm by the gallon.'

'He and Diana were well suited. They had everything.'

'Not quite,' Johnny said slowly. 'Dee always wanted a daughter.'

'Instead she got two sons. How are the boys?' Orla asked after a pause. 'Theo's done well for himself, I believe?'

'So has Sim. He's an accountant.'

Orla arched an eyebrow. 'Hardly Diana's scene.'

'He tries to keep her finances on the straight and narrow but she's as extravagant as she ever was. I don't think she'll ever change.'

'Are you still in love with her?'

'You never fall out of love with Dee. She's part of my life but every so often we have to give each other a bit of space. That's why I decided to come over and visit. It's ages since I had a proper break, so here I am.'

'What's the real reason you're here, Johnny?' Orla asked. 'And don't tell me it's for the golf or the fishing. You can do those things in England.'

'Did you receive the photograph I emailed you?'

'Yes.'

'You didn't reply.'

'I didn't know how to.'

A burst of laughter drew their attention towards the harbour and they watched as a man and a young girl fought over whose turn it was to ride a bicycle. Their feet slipped on the cobblestones and they clung on to each other to stop themselves from falling over.

'Will you look at the pair of them?' Orla said with a smile. 'It's just a game. They're not really interested in the bicycle. They want an excuse to put their arms round each other.'

'You haven't answered my question,' Johnny said.

'Do you think the girl in the photograph is Caitlin?'

'Is that the name you gave her?'

'It wasn't official, but I had to call her something and to me she looked like a Caitlin. It was my mother's name.'

'She looks like you, Orla.'

She shook her head. 'It's too much of a coincidence, Johnny. Why should my daughter bowl up on Diana's doorstep out of the blue? So the girl has red hair and mermaid eyes . . . '

'Mermaid what?' Johnny screwed up his face. 'What sort of nonsense is that?'

'It's not nonsense, it's folklore.'

'I don't know about any of that, but I can tell you I got the shock of my life when the wind swept her out of the night and into Dee's kitchen like one of your distressed mermaids. Had a bit of a job not staring at her like a goldfish. It was like turning the clock back.'

'Is this girl really that much like me?'

'She is. Luckily Dee was late as usual and I managed to hustle her out of the house before she sussed anything but truth be told I think she had her suspicions too. Molly was struck by the likeness as well.'

'You haven't answered my question. What would this girl be doing at Waterside Cottage?'

'Officially she turned up to interview Dee, but there was a bit of a mix up, something to do with Molly getting in a tangle with the arrangements. Anyway Abbie's now cataloguing Dee's memorabilia for the book she's writing. She's staying over for a while. The thing is,' Johnny shifted in his canvas chair, 'like you I thought the whole thing was a coincidence until Bethan mentioned a brooch.'

Orla adjusted the sleeve of her aquamarine blouse.

'Stop fiddling with that button,' Johnny snapped, 'and tell me what you think.'

'About what?'

'The brooch,' Johnny's voice was raised in exasperation.

'Have you seen it?'

'That's just the thing. Abbie says she can't find it. Says it's packed up with all her stuff or some such nonsense, but it can't be. Bethan saw it on her first night. They were in the study together and Bethan caught Abbie looking at it.'

'Can Bethan describe it?'

'I didn't like to press her. She says it was shaped like a star and shiny, but the thing is Abbie told Bethan her mother gave it to her. Now I know for a fact her father was a country vicar and her mother was a care assistant. She told me and people on those sorts of wages don't have diamond brooches as family heirlooms, do they?'

'Aren't you rather jumping to too

many conclusions, Johnny?'

'Am I? You saw her photo, what do you think?'

Orla's eyes clouded. How she wished Johnny hadn't sent her that photo. How she wished Abbie hadn't so resembled the pictures Orla had seen of her own mother as a young girl. The resemblance was unmistakeable. But too many hearts had been broken, too many hopes raised, then dashed.

While her father had been alive, Orla hadn't wanted to trace her daughter, the child she had given up for adoption.

It would have broken his heart to know she had given birth to a child outside of marriage, even if the child had been a much longed for granddaughter.

Then later when views on that sort of thing relaxed it had seemed best to leave the past where it belonged, in the past. Orla decided no good would come of going over what had happened so long ago.

Orla still couldn't forget how Diana

had never forgiven Orla for what had happened and they had never spoken to each other again after she had left Waterside Cottage.

'Orla?'

Johnny's voice drew her back to the present.

'It's lovely to see you again, Johnny,' she said, forcing a smile. 'I wish you'd have told me you were planning a visit, we could have gone out and about together.' She shrugged. 'As it is, I don't have the time. It's coming up to our busy season and everybody wants a part of the old Ireland. I have to be here. The youngsters I employ are good and full of enthusiasm but I can't leave them in charge. It wouldn't be fair.'

'I get it,' Johnny nodded. 'You're telling me to let sleeping dogs lie?'

Orla put out a hand and laid it on Johnny's arm. 'If Abbie is,' she hesitated, 'Caitlin, then she'll find out about it with no help from me and if she isn't, we would have stirred up a whole lot of unnecessary trouble for ourselves.'

'Don't you want to see her again?' Johnny asked and his question took Orla's breath away.

'A day hasn't gone by,' she ignored the stabbing pain in her chest as she forced herself to say, 'when I haven't thought about her. She was my only child, my beautiful perfect daughter, but I don't have the right to call myself her mother. Her mother was the wonderful woman who woke up in the middle of the night and went to her when she cried, and cuddled her when she was unwell and looked after her childhood needs. Her mother was the person she ran to when she fell over and grazed her knees.'

A lone tear trickled down Orla's cheeks. 'The person who moulded her into the beautiful young woman she is today. That woman was her mother, not me. You don't know the times I wished it didn't have to be like that.' The mermaid eyes were now swimming with tears, 'but it was and there is absolutely nothing I am going to do about it.'

'My dear girl,' Johnny's voice was hoarse with compassion. 'Am I a stupid insensitive interfering old fool or what? I had no idea. You're perfectly right, life isn't a fairy tale, life kicks you in the ribs, it does the dirty on you when you're not expecting it and it's not always full of happy endings is it?'

'Just tell me something, Johnny,' Orla asked.

'Yes?'

'If I saw my Caitlin, is she, I mean, would I be proud of her?'

'You would indeed, my darling girl. She is absolutely one of the most beautiful girls I know.'

'Then we have our happy ending, don't we?' she patted Johnny's hand.

Johnny put down his cup of tea. 'Instead of tea and mints, I suggest we take a walk down to the harbour and get ourselves something a bit stronger by way of refreshment. Then I further suggest we indulge in one of these Irish evenings you've been banging on about and if my feet aren't aching from dancing by the end of the evening, I shall want to know why.'

Johnny dragged Orla to her feet. 'Come on. I don't intend waiting around for ever.'

'Why could you and I never get together, Johnny?' Orla asked touching his cheek tenderly.

'Because we would have driven each other up the wall in seconds. Meeting up once every twenty years or so is about as much as we could handle don't you think?'

'Do you know, Johnny,' Orla laughed, 'I think you're absolutely right. Come on then, a night of dancing it is.'

Theo And Sim Compete For Abbie

'Darling, it is far too hot in here. You'll fry your brain.' Diana swanned into the study leaving the door wide open and crossing to the windows flung them open with one elegant flick of her wrist.

'No,' Abbie called out, but her warning was too late. Her carefully arranged piles of papers and photos caught in the cross draught flew all over the floor.

Diana made a face. 'Sorry,' she apologised, 'here let me help.'

'Don't touch anything.' Abbie had great difficulty not shouting at Diana. It had taken her most of the morning to create some order out of the chaos of Diana's photos and in one minute Diana had demolished a day's work.

'Go on,' Diana urged, 'you know you

want to.' Her almond shaped eyes twinkled with mischief.

'Want to what?' Abbie ground at her through gritted teeth as she began chasing bits of paper round the floor. 'Can't you shut the window a bit?' she demanded.

'You want to tell me I'm a selfish, self-centred, spoilt creature, who only ever thinks of herself. Why on earth did I have to storm in here and disrupt you when you were getting along so nicely without me?'

Abbie was furious with Diana but despite her annoyance it was difficult to be really cross with her. She had the infuriating habit of being one step ahead and despite her outrageous behaviour she was always genuinely repentant afterwards.

'That's better. I like it when you smile.' Diana beamed back at her. 'And you're perfectly right. I'm very very sorry and I humbly apologise. There, are we friends again?' She held out her hands in a gesture of contrition.

'Diana, you really are . . . ' Abbie struggled to find the right word.

'I know, darling. I always have been, but you see I'm not good at doing nothing, and with Johnny away in Ireland, there's no one to play with. I suppose you don't fancy a day out?'

'You employed me to sort out this mess.' Abbie swept a hand over the desk, 'not to take days off at the drop of a hat.'

'And it's outrageous of me to distract you.' Diana slumped down on the window seat. 'If only I hadn't had that silly argument with Johnny and then Molly's not speaking to me either, did you know that?'

'Again?' Abbie was hardly listening. It was a way of life at Waterside Cottage. Molly and Diana were either best of friends, or daggers drawn.

'I don't make a habit of arguing with my mother,' Diana flared up. 'How dare you suggest otherwise?'

Abbie took a deep breath. Diana was clearly in one of her moods and wanting to stir things up. If she weren't careful Abbie would find herself in a situation she couldn't control. Diana would probably have one of her famed hissy fits and sack Abbie on the spot then she would be out of a job and homeless.

'Theo mentioned something about collecting Bethan from school. It's a half day for teacher training. Why don't you go and meet them?'

As a diversionary tactic it was an instant success. Diana leapt to her feet and clapped her hands. 'You are a clever girl. That's exactly what I'll do. I know,' she warmed to the idea, 'if I take the car, we can go on somewhere later. Bethan loves ice cream and I think there's a fair in the village. Theo's bound to be a bit of an attraction. You can look after your own lunch and tea can't you if we get delayed?'

'I think so,' Abbie replied with a wry smile. Since arriving at Waterside Cottage catering arrangements had been on the sketchy side and most evenings she fended for herself with Theo arriving back at the last minute and offering to help when all the work was done.

His presence had created an added problem for Abbie. Far from being the help he had promised, he was a serious distraction, Not a day passed when the telephone didn't ring. It was usually for Theo and the callers nearly always female.

Abbie sat back on her heels as Diana glided out of the study leaving only a trace of the floral perfume she favoured. It had been especially created for her by one of the French perfume houses, when she had played the role of Lady Alexandra and she had continued wearing it after the series had finished.

It suited Diana's character perfectly. It was subtle, expensive and chic with a dash of mystery all thrown in. Abbie chewed her lip.

Despite Diana's charm Abbie's journalistic intuition told her she was hiding a part of her life. Abbie's limited experience of celebrities had led her to believe most of them only revealed so much of their characters, the bits they wanted you to know about but on more occasions than not there was always another side, one they kept hidden away.

What could Diana have to hide? Her life had been well documented first as the daughter of the famed sportsman, Sir Justin LaTrobe, then in her own right as a very successful actress. Also her first marriage to Don Foxton was constant celebrity magazine gossip fodder. Books had been written about her and a publisher had commissioned her memoirs too. That left little scope for a hidden past.

Abbie frowned — except for the brooch. She still hadn't had a chance to discover why she had found Diana's diamond brooch amongst her father's effects. After Bethan had blurted out about it over the lunch table Abbie hadn't dared look at it again.

Johnny Cavendish had asked to see it

once or twice and so far Abbie had managed to fob him off, but for how much longer? She could only put her reluctance to show it to him down to her fear that she might be stirring up a hornet's nest.

If her father's past was inexplicably linked in some way to Diana's did she really want to know? Abbie wasn't sure any more.

Now her concentration was broken, she couldn't help thinking about Diana. It was strange Johnny taking off for Ireland at short notice.

According to Diana she had been caught speeding while driving Johnny's car and when he had received the notice of the infringement he had been furious with her. As a reason for an argument it sounded a bit flimsy to Abbie.

All the same Johnny had packed himself off to Ireland allegedly to do some fishing and play a bit of golf.

Abbie stirred herself. She'd better get on. For the moment the brooch must stay where she had hidden it — under a small beam in her bedroom. It had been a wise precaution putting it where no one would find it. Whilst she was sure none of the Foxtons would stoop so low as to searching her room, it could be embarrassing if someone discovered it accidentally while they were doing something as simple as returning her bag or an article of clothing.

Life was a tad bohemian at Waterside Cottage and Diana thought nothing of borrowing a cardigan if it was lying around or a jacket, no matter whom it belonged to. On more than one occasion Abbie had discovered Diana in her bedroom returning items of her clothing.

'Anybody at home?' a voice called down the hall.

'In here,' Abbie replied.

Sim Foxton nudged open the study door. 'Good heavens what on earth's been going on here?'

He surveyed the papers strewn across

the floor. 'Is this the new business method way of working?'

'No it is not,' Abbie retaliated, pleased to have a scapegoat to round on. 'Your mother . . . '

Sim held up a hand. 'Say no more. Want some help?'

He ventured into the room then stepped back dramatically, reeling from the expression on Abbie's face.

'Did I say something wrong?' he asked. 'Or do you normally bare your teeth when people offer to help with your work?'

'Your mother offered to help.'

'She created havoc in my office. Wiped off a spreadsheet when she was playing with the computer keyboard. Luckily we had a backup but she was not flavour of the month that day, I can tell you. If it's any consolation, she doesn't mean to and she's always very sorry afterwards.' Sim's slow smile did its usual trick of setting Abbie's pulses racing.

'Tell me about it,' Abbie said raising her eyes. 'If you're looking for Diana, by the way, then you're out of luck. She isn't here. You've just missed her. She's taking Theo and Bethan to the fair for the afternoon.'

A look of annoyance replaced the smile on Sim's face. 'If that isn't the pits. We had an appointment this lunchtime.'

'Do you normally make an appointment to see your mother?' Abbie asked.

'It was a business meeting. I wanted to go through some accounts with her.' Sim strode to the desk and flipped open the leather bound book. 'Here it is. Twelve o'clock.'

'I don't think Diana ever looks at the diary, does she?'

'Then you should have reminded her.'

'Now hold on,' Abbie protested, 'I'm not her secretary. Molly's supposed to see to all that.'

'And when did any of us last see my grandmother?'

Abbie felt the beginnings of laughter bubble up inside her. The situation was too ridiculous for words.

'What is so funny?' Sim demanded, scowling at Abbie.

'I so know where you're coming from.'

Sim's glare faded into a conciliatory smile of resignation.

'Sorry. I always seem to take it out on you when my family let me down, don't I?'

'Yes you do.'

Abbie saw no reason to let Sim off lightly. 'Your family's behaviour is not my fault or my responsibility.'

'Fancy a sandwich or something for lunch?' Sim asked. 'You look like you need a break.'

Abbie glanced at the sheets of paper littering the floor.

'All right,' she agreed. 'I think there's some cheese in the fridge if you're interested.'

★　★　★

'So,' Sim chewed on his cheddar and tomato sandwich, 'what made you take up journalism?'

'It took me up really,' Abbie replied.

In the warmth of the kitchen with the back door open letting in the spring sunshine, Abbie could almost convince herself her suspicions about the Foxtons hiding a dark secret was unfounded. So what if they were a little theatrical? That went with the territory. It was natural Molly and Diana should have differences of opinion. They were both highly volatile, strong-minded women and in that aspect they were no different from many a mother and daughter.

As for Theo and Sim they both had responsible jobs; and Theo especially, with his artistic temperament, needed a release valve.

'Did you win a school prize for essay writing or something?' Sim asked.

Abbie smiled. It was a story she loved telling. 'Actually it was a way of bunking off school. I used to help edit the parish magazine and my father was very forward thinking. He liked to have as much local input as possible in every edition, so in order to develop my social skills, and with my head teacher's approval, I'd cycle round the village asking people if they'd been to the flower show or what they thought of the proposed increased parking fees, anything of that nature really.'

'Smart move,' Sim acknowledged, 'wish I'd have thought of something similar to get out of lessons at school.'

'You didn't fancy following your mother into acting?'

A look of horror crossed Sim's face. 'I can think of nothing worse than standing in front of a camera spouting someone else's words.'

'Then you haven't inherited your mother's genes?'

Sim hesitated. 'I don't think so. I've always liked figures, you know where you are with them so I passed my exams then set up a practice of my own.' A dimple dented Sim's cheek. 'Do you realise this is the first civilised conversation we've had?'

'That's because you spread rumours

about me to the family.'

'I do not,' Sim objected.

'Yes you do. You told Molly I wasn't coming back after she gave me an advance on my salary.'

'As usual, the family gossip machine seems to have got things a bit confused.'

'So you deny it?'

'I admit I did express some concern that Molly had parted with such a large sum of money, but I don't think I went so far as to blacken your name. If that's the impression you got then I'm sorry.'

'I suppose I can't blame you for thinking like that,' Abbie admitted reluctant to acknowledge she was growing to like Sim more every time she met him. 'I mean, you didn't really know anything about me and I could have been a sophisticated con woman, sorry I mean person.'

'I'm so glad you weren't.'

'Am I interrupting anything?' A voice sliced the atmosphere between them.

A frown of annoyance crossed Sim's

face as he looked up at Theo.

'What are you doing here?' he demanded, 'I thought you were wooing the local girls at the village fete.

'Then you thought wrong.' Theo sauntered into the kitchen and helped himself to a chunk of cheddar and a tomato. 'I decided I'm a little too old for hoopla stalls and guessing the weight of the Victoria sponge, besides which,' he smiled lazily at Abbie, 'Diana's in her element, signing autographs and generally showing off and there's only so much of that I can take. So I decided to come back to Waterside Cottage and invite Abbie out to a party this evening.'

After Johnny's revelation about Theo stealing Sim's fiancée away from him, Abbie had been at pains not to be alone with Theo.

She didn't want to give Sim more reason to distrust her.

'In that case as we've finished our lunch,' Sim stood up, 'I'll leave you to it.'

'Don't go on my account,' Theo drawled. 'Or is it me who's in the way?'

His eyes moved from Sim to Abbie and Abbie had the feeling he was enjoying himself. She bit down her frustration. What a family of trouble-makers they were.

'I think I should get back to work too,' she said firmly. 'I'll tell Diana you called,' she spoke to Sim, 'when she gets back.'

'If she gets back,' Sim muttered. 'She's quite likely not to reappear for hours.'

'Surely she wouldn't leave Bethan,' Abbie protested.

'Bethan'll be fine. She will probably go for a ride on Paddy. It's what she usually does on her days off school.' Theo waved aside any concern Abbie might have for his daughter. 'Now what about this party invitation? It's tonight and it's dress casual.'

'I don't think so,' Abbie replied.

'But Molly especially wants you to come. She told me to make sure you got an invitation. She hasn't thrown a party in ages. We're all congregating on the canal at eight and it's going to be a warm evening so you won't freeze your fingers off. Say you'll come?' Theo pleaded. 'Of course you're included in the invite too, Sim.' Theo's voice sounded anything but inviting.

'Actually Susannah and I are having dinner with her parents tonight,' Sim replied.

'Ah yes and how is the lovely Susannah?' Theo asked.

'She's very well,' Sim clipped back at him.

'I'd like to meet up with her again. Tell you what, why don't you and Susannah drop into Molly's party after dinner with her parents? It's bound to go on late and that way,' he cast a glance at Abbie, 'you could introduce the girls to each other. I'm sure you'd like to meet Sim's girlfriend wouldn't you, Abbie?'

Sim picked up his car keys off the table. 'We'll see,' was all he said.

'Glad he's gone,' Theo stage whispered as Sim strode out of the kitchen. 'Now we can have the whole afternoon to ourselves. What do you suggest we do?'

Abbie Feels Like One
Of The Family

Neither Bethan nor Diana had returned to Waterside Cottage by the time Theo and Abbie decided to start walking down the towpath. A hurried teatime telephone call from Diana had informed Abbie they were staying on for the pre-teen disco.

'Bethan's friend is here,' Diana informed her as she picked up the telephone, 'and I am in sore need of a party. There's a grown-up do next door, chez some old chums of mine, Felicity and Guy, so expect us when you see us.'

'Good,' Theo had replied when Abbie had relayed the contents of the telephone call to him, 'that leaves us free to make our own way to Molly's party.'

* * *

Fairy lights twinkled like little lanterns on Molly's canal boat and Theo and Abbie could hear heavy metal music and laughter drifting upstream towards them on the clear evening air.

'Looks like Molly's get-together is up to her usual standard,' Theo commented, as there was a loud splash from the water. 'Wonder who or what's fallen in this time.'

'Does she often give parties?' Abbie asked. She was beginning to think she might regret having accepted Molly's invitation if things were going to get out of hand.

'She hasn't had one since her birthday so I suppose you could say one's overdue.' Theo linked his fingers through Abbie's and squeezed her hand. 'There's no need to look so worried. I'll take care of you and the Foxtons always keep their word.'

Abbie would have liked to snatch her hand out of Theo's grasp but it would have seemed churlish after all the help he had given her that afternoon.

Contrary to her fears they had actually got down to some serious work after lunch. Theo had been a great help chronicling Diana's photographs and they had made quite a bit of headway with her film pictures too.

'I used to love visiting the studios,' Theo explained as he input the latest data into the computer. 'Can't remember much about it, but there was a lovely Irish girl there who always let me play in her workroom. She used to ply me with sweets and sing love ballads to me. I've always had a thing about red hair ever since.'

Abbie had turned her attention back to the albums, not wanting Theo to get ideas about running his fingers through her auburn hair. He had chuckled as if reading her mind before picking up another photo.

'You know, you're turning out to be quite a slave driver,' he complained with a twinkle in his eye as they walked

140

along the towpath. 'I haven't worked so hard since I was made to cram for my exams at school.'

'Did you pass?' Abbie asked, more for anything to say that a genuine desire to know the answer.

'Actually I did, second time around,' he replied, 'with honours. I can do the work, but I'm lazy. Can't stand being indoors. Show me a river to cross or a forest to explore and I'm your man, but sitting in a stuffy room revising brings me out in hives.'

'You and Sim are very different characters, aren't you?'

'I suppose we are. His idea of pleasure is a long list of figures to add up,' Theo shuddered, 'my idea of hell. Now no more questions about Sim, or I shall get jealous and we are here to party,' he said as they approached the gaily-lit canal boat.

The movement created by the extra passengers on board was creating small waves in the water and the sound of them slapping the side of the boat reminded Abbie of her evening walks along the sea front outside her parents' bungalow.

'Jolly Molly,' Theo called out, 'permission to come aboard?'

Molly was on deck and dressed in an outlandish silk catsuit of orange swirls decorated with green leaves. Abbie blinked. She was also sporting huge orange-rimmed glasses to match and atop her grey hair was a jaunty orange baseball cap proclaiming the words, *Admiral of the Fleet.*

'Abbie, my pet,' she kissed her on the cheek. 'You got her here, Theo, well done. Now listen up everyone, the guest of honour has arrived.'

Abbie looked round in alarm at the sea of faces all smiling at her. Some had painted faces in weird shades of silver and gold. Others were dressed in black clothes decorated with studs. On the walk down she had noticed several motorbikes parked alongside the towpath and assumed they belonged to Molly's biker crowd.

'Molly,' she hissed, a frisson of fear working its way up her backbone, 'what have you been up to?'

'Dear girl,' her glasses moved as she widened her eyes, 'you've been with us how long now?'

'Ten days.'

'Exactly, an age and no one has officially welcomed you to the family. I call that outrageous, don't you?' She addressed her remark to her surrounding guests. There was a general murmur of agreement.

'Nice one, Moll,' one of the bikers raised his glass to Abbie. 'Welcome to the Hamwater Chapter, Abbie, may you never run out of engine oil.'

A ragged cheer greeted his words.

'So this party is in your honour and, ta da,' Molly sang out with an enthusiastic sweep of her hands, 'I have made you a cake.'

Theo groaned. 'Please tell me it's not one of your specials, Molly. The last one sank like a stone.'

Precariously placed on a small table

in the far corner of the deck was a rather wobbly-looking affair composed of three tiers, the top tier of which looked in danger of collapsing. It was badly iced in lurid pink and perched crookedly on top was the figure of a female with bright red hair.

'Do you like it?' Molly asked anxiously. 'I'm not very good at baking but I did my best and I tried to ice the word 'welcome' on the bottom bit, but the icing kept running so I gave up.'

It was a few moments before Abbie could reply. 'I absolutely love it.' She smiled into Molly's sweet face and the bikers cheered and stomped their approval again.

'Bet it'll taste disgusting,' Theo murmured in Abbie's ear. 'Cake making and Molly are words that do not go into the same sentence.'

'I heard that,' Molly glared at him, 'and I'll have you know I sat up half the night preparing it.'

'And I am very grateful.' Abbie felt a silly lump blocking her throat. The idea of Molly working into the small hours decorating her wobbly cake was incredibly touching and she was determined to eat a slice if only for Molly's sake.

A loud burst of laughter at the far end of the boat interrupted them. 'I'd better go and find out what's going on at the helm. Help yourself to a drink,' Molly said, 'we've got everything — nibbles and nuts down in the galley. Party won't finish until sunrise or until the police are called, whichever happens first.'

With a flash of orange silk Molly disappeared towards the sound of the laughter that was steadily growing more raucous.

'She is joking?' Abbie asked anxiously.

'I hope so,' Theo replied. 'Come on, let's see what we can find in the way of eats. I am starving.'

Half an hour later after jockeying for food in the confines of Molly's cabin and clutching lurid coloured drinks Theo and Abbie clambered off the Jolly

Molly and back on to the towpath.

'That's better.' Theo breathed a sigh of relief. 'What a crush down there. I never do seem to get my sea legs on the Jolly Molly. Think there's something wrong with her stabilisers. Do canal boats have them?'

Abbie shook her head. 'I don't know.'

'Probably my funny insides, then.' Theo pulled a face. 'Don't tell anyone will you? Wouldn't do my publicity any good if the papers get hold of the story. I can see the headlines now. Theo Foxton gets seasick on his granny's paddleboat. Can you imagine the havoc that would cause?'

Abbie laughed. 'I won't tell a soul,' she promised.

★ ★ ★

Despite her initial fears Abbie was enjoying herself. Theo had proved an excellent companion and had stayed glued to her side ever since they had arrived. He had introduced her to those

146

of Molly's guests who he knew and the ones he didn't know lost no time in making themselves known to Abbie.

'Biker Chapter Three,' one tattooed man had shaken her hand and almost broken her fingers. 'Any time you fancy a spin, I'm on to your case. Any friend of Moll's is a friend of mine. She's a great girl.'

Abbie knew she would never remember all the names, but no one seemed too bothered about formal introductions and she had had several more rally invitations pressed on her and the offer of a pillion ride to a rock festival in the summer.

'If you want to mingle, Theo,' Abbie began with a face that ached from so much smiling. She collapsed on to a wooden bench.

'Wouldn't dream of deserting you,' Theo insisted, nibbling at a cocktail sausage.

'I won't mind. You've been an excellent host so feel free to do your own thing.'

Theo cast her a sideways glance as he swallowed the last of his sausage. 'Actually, if you're sure,' he began with a shamefaced smile, 'I did spot an old girlfriend or two I'd quite like to catch up with.'

'Then go right ahead,' Abbie stifled a yawn. 'It's been a long day and I am beginning to wilt. I'll sit here for a while and rest up.'

'Come and find me if you want to go home and I'll walk you back.'

'Will do.'

She watched Theo uncurl his long legs and stand up. He liked to dress well and despite the casual dress code of the party he was wearing tailored chinos and an exclusive designer polo shirt that Abbie recognised as being well out of her price range.

Of the two brothers, Theo was by far and away the most handsome. Theo was like a peacock. He had to be admired, by the more females the better. She watched as females, bikers with painted faces and pretty party girls

gravitated towards him. Soon an adoring circle agog to hear of his latest
exploits surrounded him.

Abbie's lips curved into a reluctant
smile. The Foxtons were an impossibly
charismatic family and she knew she
would need to keep her head in order
to stop herself from being seduced by
their glamour.

With a twinge of guilt she remembered she was at Waterside Cottage
under slightly false pretences, even
though she was doing a job of work.
Now she was beginning to come to
grips with the cataloguing of Diana's
photographs, she knew she ought to do
something about the brooch, but what?
It would be too hurtful to rake up old
scandals — if there was one.

And how could she hurt Molly after
she had gone to all the trouble of
arranging a party and her loving gesture
of making a cake? Despite Molly's
youthful vigour, her hands were not as
agile as they had once been and Abbie
appreciated how difficult it must have

been for her to stay up half the night trying to ice her cake.

Should Abbie abandon her quest to get at the truth? So what if Diana had a secret in her past? Didn't everyone? What right did Abbie have to unearth it? Everyone had been more than kind to her at Waterside Cottage. She couldn't throw their hospitality back in their faces. It would be too cruel.

The sound of approaching footsteps along the towpath drew Abbie's attention away from the water.

Sim was walking towards her arm in arm with a girl who she could only guess was Susannah. She was wearing a plain white shift dress and her cascading blonde hair was held back away from her face in a floppy velvet bow making Abbie feel dowdy in comparison in her chain store summer dress.

'Hello,' she stood up. 'I'm getting a breath of fresh air. Molly's friends certainly know how to party.'

'Where's Theo?' Sim asked.

Susannah's feline eyes strayed in the

direction of The Jolly Molly. 'I think you'll find he's over there,' she drawled.

'Yes,' Abbie smiled, 'with all his old girlfriends and judging by the look of things, he's adoring every moment of it.'

'So,' Susannah's smile didn't quite reach her eyes. 'You're the hired help?'

Temporarily lost for words at Susannah's description of her job, Abbie didn't reply. It was left to Sim to make the introductions.

'Abbie Rogers, Susannah Green.'

'Darling.' An orange typhoon of colour appeared from nowhere. 'It's so good to see you. Give your old Molly a kiss.'

Sim stooped forward and dutifully embraced his grandmother. 'What on earth are you wearing?' He eyed up her outfit.

'Don't you like it?'

'It's very vibrant.'

'Wicked,' Molly beamed at him. 'I wanted to make an impression.'

'You've certainly done that,' Sim

replied with a wry twist to his lips. 'Where are my dark glasses?'

'Don't be impertinent,' Molly scolded him. 'I suppose that mother of yours still isn't talking to me?' she asked. 'Honestly such a fuss about — do you know I can't even remember what we argued about now. Tell her I'll call at the house tomorrow. I need to use the washing machine.'

'She's actually having dinner with my parents,' Susannah interrupted Molly's flow.

Abbie could only describe the look Molly gave Susannah as lukewarm.

'Hello, Susannah.' Molly straightened her baseball cap, which had slipped to a rakish angle when she'd embraced Sim. 'I'm afraid I haven't invited anyone important for you to network with. I'll understand if you don't want to stay.'

'That's all right, Molly.' Susannah's response was equally cool. 'I'll stay on at your little party for a while. I'll go and talk to Theo. It's been a while since I've seen him.' She unlinked arms with

Sim and strolled over to Theo's group. Moments later the two of them were embracing warmly. Abbie couldn't help noticing the triumphant glance Susannah threw in Sim's direction.

'If I wasn't a lady,' Molly said, 'I would tell you exactly what I think of that girl, Sim.'

'It's never stopped you before from voicing your opinion on my girlfriends,' Sim replied.

'That's because I didn't like any of 'em,' was Molly's robust reply.

Fearing another situation might be about to develop, Abbie butted in. 'Molly made me a delicious cake.'

Abbie couldn't have wished for a better reaction to her diversion tactic.

'You what?' Sim's expression was a mixture of disbelief, horror and amusement. 'You didn't eat any of it, did you?'

'Not yet, but I'm going to have a slice later,' Abbie said.

'I shouldn't,' Molly said, a resigned look on her face.

'Why ever not?' Abbie asked.

'I'm not sure it's cooked properly and I have to confess someone picked it up and well, it sort of collapsed,' Molly admitted. 'I think if I hadn't been looking they'd have thrown it overboard. No, darling,' Molly stroked her arm, 'flattered as I am by your kindness, you're better off sticking with the cocktail sausages. Now, Sim, what would you like to drink?'

'Nothing thanks. Susannah's parents are very good hosts and I think I've had sufficient for one night.'

'That's a lovely dress Susannah's wearing,' Abbie said as they looked across to where she was still standing arm-in-arm with Theo.

'Yours is much nicer,' Molly said. 'Doesn't that blue bring out the colour in Abbie's eyes, Sim?'

'Yes' he said softly, 'it does.'

Abbie began to feel uncomfortable under their scrutiny. 'Freelance journalists don't get much chance to dress up,' she said, 'this is my best dress.'

'Then I'm honoured you wore it for our little party.'

'Molly?' a voice bellowed from the deck, as there was another loud splash, 'cake overboard.'

'I knew it,' she said triumphantly. 'Someone's arranged a convenient accident. How very thoughtful of them. Now, Abbie darling, there will be no need for you to pretend to eat a slice. Better go and see how much mess they've made. Hope they haven't brained a passing duck. Look after Abbie won't you, Sim. Theo seems to have abandoned her.'

'There's no need to look after me,' Abbie said once Molly was out of earshot.

'Why do you persist in avoiding my company?' Sim asked.

'I don't,' Abbie protested.

'Yes you do. I don't bite.'

'Look I don't know the state of your relationship with Susannah, but I really don't want to disrupt things.'

'You won't,' Sim replied looking over

to where his brother still had his arm around Susannah's shoulders. 'Theo's already got it in hand.'

'Why do you let him steal your girlfriends?' Abbie asked in frustration remembering the story Johnny had told her about Sim's fiancée.

'Perhaps because I haven't met the right girl — until now.'

Abbie was glad it was too dark for Sim to see the expression in her eyes. What exactly had he meant by that last remark? She cleared her throat.

'Theo's promised to walk me home and I'm about ready to go.'

'Theo won't be ready to leave for hours yet,' Sim said.

'Then I don't want to drag him away. I'd better say a quick goodbye to Molly.'

'I'll join you.'

'But you've only just arrived and you can't leave Susannah.'

The fairy lights from The Jolly Molly turned Sim's eyes from gentle golden brown to a harsher hue. 'I'm sure I can entrust her to Theo's care.' He hesitated. 'By the way, I'm sorry about earlier.'

'Earlier?'

'Susannah should never have referred to you as the hired help.'

'It's what I am, I suppose,' Abbie admitted with a laugh. 'I don't mind you know. I've been called a lot worse in my career.'

'Not by me,' his voice was soft. 'You don't object to my company on the walk back?'

'If you're sure you want to leave?'

'I want to leave,' Sim replied. 'There's only so much of Molly's music that I can take, and,' he added, a small muscle quivering at the corner of his mouth, 'the prospect of a moonlit walk home with the beautiful Abbie Rogers is enough to make any man's pulses race.'

Abbie caught her breath in surprise then laughed at the teasing expression in his eyes. It had been such a silly thing to say and if he had been Theo she probably would have hugged him. But the idea of flinging her arm around Sim Foxton was not a move she trusted herself to make.

Instead she contented herself with, 'In that case, how could a girl possibly refuse such a charming invitation?'

Sim Gets Closer To Abbie

'You could claim a chauffeur as a legitimate allowance,' Sim was patiently trying to explain the situation to Diana, but she was in no mood to listen.

'I tried to tell that officious policeman that the speed limit always used to be forty along that stretch of road and that I hadn't noticed the new signs and why on earth had they changed it to thirty anyway, but all he said was ignorance was no excuse and that I was still booked.'

She paused for dramatic effect. 'You don't seem to realise the seriousness of the situation, Sim,' Diana said, when he looked singularly unimpressed by this piece of news. 'This is the third time I have been stopped for speeding in a month. I shall probably lose my licence.'

'I understand perfectly. All I'm saying

is . . . ' Sim tried to raise his voice above that of Diana's, but his mother's theatrical training had the edge and with a wry look at Abbie he gave up trying to interrupt her.

Only the night noises from the river had interrupted the intimacy of their walk home. After the recent rain, the undergrowth smelt damp and the towpath was littered with the confetti of fallen cherry blossom.

'Those shoes don't look a very sensible choice for a riverside walk,' Sim had said as the heel of one of Abbie's strappy sandals threatened to part company with the rest of the shoe.

'I could hardly wear trainers to a party,' Abbie retaliated, 'and since we're on the subject of dress, is a suit with collar and tie a sensible choice for a party?'

'It is when you're having dinner with Guy and Felicity.' Sim wrenched his tie away from his collar and undid the top buttons of his shirt. 'That's better. They always make those things far too tight for comfort. Now where was I?'

'You were giving me your expert opinion on my choice of footwear,' Abbie said trying to ignore his gaping collar and the fine down of hair exposed by the undone shirt buttons.

'It was only an excuse for me to hold your hand,' Sim admitted, a dimple denting his cheek as he smiled at her.

'I'm not falling for that one and neither am I some soppy teenager with stars in her eyes,' Abbie protested, 'so no you can't — hold my hand.'

'How old are you?' Sim asked.

'Twenty-five. How old are you?'

'I'm thirty.'

'Then you're far too old to play love's young dream as well, aren't you?'

'Yes,' Sim agreed, entwining his fingers around hers.

'What are you doing?' Abbie demanded.

'It gets very slippery on this part of the footpath and if I'm going to slide over I fully intend taking you with me.'

'How very gallant of you.'

'It's what the Foxtons are noted for

— their chivalry.'

The sensation of Sim's warm hand in hers gave Abbie the feeling of security, but for all she knew Sim was practised in this sort of behaviour.

It virtually went with the territory when you were a Foxton. The two brothers only had to click their fingers to have half the girls in the district running after them.

'Well the Rogers aren't into chivalry so if you take a tumble, then you're on your own.'

'Why did I suspect you might come back at me with an answer like that?' Sim asked with a resigned sigh.

'Because I am a modern, independent minded woman who has seen far too much of life to fall for a silver tongued smooth delivery like that. Besides which you have a girlfriend — or had you conveniently forgotten about the lovely Susannah?'

'I think when Theo's around she forgets about me,' Sim said quietly. 'It's not the first time it's happened.'

Abbie bit her lip. She still wasn't sure of the history of the fiancée Sim had lost to Theo. Had he married her and was she Bethan's mother?

'Isn't that Diana's car?' Abbie had asked as they ducked under the trees surrounding Waterside Cottage and made their way up the path to the house.

It was indeed Diana's roadster, slewed to an angry angle in the forecourt and the intimate atmosphere created between Sim and Abbie on their walk home along the river had totally evaporated when they pushed open the door to the study to find Diana pacing the room and ready to go on the rampage.

'Where've you been?' she demanded.

'What's happened?' Sim demanded taking in the scenario.

'You may well ask.' Diana's eyelashes worked overtime to keep up with the speed of her emotion. 'Johnny is away. Like the rest of you he has deserted me. He has swanned over to Ireland, so he can't drive me around and I dare not risk more points on my licence. Stuck out here I have to have transport. This is all your fault.' She glared at Sim.

'Mine?' Sim raised his eyebrows with a comical look of dismay on his face. 'How can whatever is wrong be my fault?'

'If you hadn't insisted on leaving Guy and Felicity's early to go to Molly's ghastly party none of this would have happened.'

Sim cast a faintly embarrassed glance in Abbie's direction. 'It was in Abbie's honour, Diana and I had promised to put in an appearance. You should have been there too.' He frowned. 'I still don't see what is supposed to be my fault.'

'Because it was way past Bethan's bedtime.'

'No,' Sim shrugged. 'I'm still not getting it.'

'And that was why I was driving too fast.'

'Not down the hill from the golf club?'

'Bethan, the poor mite was exhausted. She'd been dancing her toes off at the disco. She's so popular,' Diana smirked as she temporarily forgot how angry she was. 'She takes after me with her natural sense of rhythm. Quite the little star she was tonight. Anyway I had to get her home. She was almost asleep on her feet.' She broke off to point an accusing finger at Sim. 'You should have brought her home when you left Guy's and not gone off gallivanting around the countryside attending parties.'

'It may have escaped your notice, Diana but Bethan is Theo's daughter, not mine and as such the child is his responsibility.'

'If I wasn't here to hold this family together, I don't know what would become of any of you.'

This was too much for Abbie. She had been struggling to keep her face straight ever since they stumbled on an

outraged Diana patrolling the study, •
but the idea of her being a modern day
Joan of Arc, sacrificing her all for the
family, was the last straw.

She burst into laughter. For a second
Diana's face was frozen in outrage as
she watched Abbie hiccup an apology
behind her hand, then a reluctant smile
tugged at the corners of the older
woman's mouth.

'I'm being impossible, aren't I?' she
acknowledged.

'Yes, you are,' Abbie admitted, liking
Diana all the more for having the
courage to own up to her bad temper,
'and I think you owe Sim an apology.'

'I'm sorry, darlings,' Diana was
instantly contrite, 'but honestly the
policeman who stopped me looked
about twelve years old. He had a sweet
little fresh face and his ears stuck out
under his cap. But you haven't heard
the best of it.' Diana's eyes were
enormous with outrage as she warmed
to her theme again. 'After he'd finished
booking me he went very red in the face

and actually had the nerve to ask me for my autograph.'

'You should have been flattered,' Sim said, 'you know you like being asked for your autograph.'

'It was for his grandmother.' Diana looked ready to explode. 'He said she never misses an episode of *Masquerade*, now they're being repeated on television and she would be thrilled to bits to know her grandson had met the famous Lady Alexandra.' Diana looked from Sim to Abbie for a reaction.

By now Sim was also having great difficulty keeping a straight face.

'Very trying, Diana,' he did his best to soothe her, 'but at least you're home and Bethan's safely tucked up in bed. So no harm done.'

Diana looked as though she would have liked to dispute this point but instead she asked, 'Did you two walk home alone from Molly's party?' There was a note of suspicion in her voice as she changed the subject.

'Yes,' Abbie replied hesitantly. 'We

were both feeling a bit tired and the party was beginning to wind down.'

'What happened to Susannah?' Diana demanded.

'She stayed behind with Theo,' Sim said.

'Honestly, Sim,' Diana raised her eyebrows. 'What am I going to do with you?'

'Now what have I done wrong?'

'The girl is crazy about you and all you can do is leave her behind at a party to walk home with Abbie. Sometimes I think you've got no more sense than you were born with.'

'We were ready to leave,' Sim replied, 'and Susannah's not the jealous sort. Besides, there's nothing to be jealous of. She and I are no more than good friends.'

'G . . . good friends?' Diana stuttered. 'Susannah is jealousy on legs and who wouldn't be jealous of your friendship with this ravishing creature?'

Abbie's ears felt as though they were on fire. Surely Diana wasn't talking about her. No one had ever described her as a ravishing creature before. One look in the mirror was always enough to convince Abbie that her looks were nothing more than homely. Her hair was her most striking feature but as she also had the temperament to go with it, it wasn't always such a blessing.

'Well, I absolutely forbid it,' Diana said.

'Forbid what?' Sim demanded.

'Any fraternisation between you and Abbie.'

'One walk home after a party does not constitute a relationship,' Sim spoke very slowly and carefully, 'and even if it did, it really is none of your business, Diana.'

'Everything that goes on under my roof is my business.'

'Then thank goodness I no longer live here,' Sim snapped. 'Now before I leave I need to make another appointment with you to go through some of your accounts for tax purposes. You seem to have forgotten the one we made for earlier today. Maybe if you hadn't, you might not be facing a driving ban now.'

'Go right ahead,' Diana said absently, running a hand through her newly low-lighted locks. 'You'd better make a note of it, Abbie. I'll never remember. When is Molly coming back? Did she say?'

'She said something about dropping by tomorrow morning,' Abbie replied, making a diplomatic decision not to mention the washing machine.

'Typical. Isn't that just like her? Wanting to swan back in as if nothing had happened.' Diana fumed. 'Well I'm not going to be the first to apologise. Some of the things she said to me a mother should never be allowed to say to her daughter.'

'Did you know you've got a voice-over booked for Friday morning?' Sim asked as he leafed through the diary.

'What?' Diana shrieked and grabbed the book out of Sim's hands. She read the entry under her breath then snapped the diary shut. 'There's nothing else for it, I'll have to cancel. I know it's unprofessional but there it is.'

'You can't cancel, Diana, you need the money.'

'In that case you'll have to drive me up there, Abbie.'

'Me?'

'Sim is right. I can't let them down. It's a promotion for a range of *Masquerade* memorabilia. With all this renewed interest in the series there's talk about a feature length special coming up too with some of the old cast. I have to be there to discuss things with the promoters.'

'I thought when you retired that was it,' Sim said.

'So did I, darling.' Diana's earlier annoyance with her elder son seemed to have evaporated, 'but I'm not very good at doing nothing,' Diana admitted, 'and there is a growing market for older female leads these days. When I left *Masquerade* the business was only looking for young twenty-somethings.

With the resurgence of the profile of the successful older woman, things have changed. Darling,' she grabbed Sim's arm, 'this could be the chance of a lifetime for me.'

'But I'm not a professional driver,' Abbie protested.

'You've got a valid licence haven't you?'

'Yes, but . . . '

Then you're appointed. I don't want a stranger driving me round the place. I know you Abbie and I trust you. I'll speak to my insurers in the morning and get your name put on the policy. Please?' She pleaded.

'But you haven't actually lost your licence have you?' Abbie had no wish to be the trusted confidante of Diana. The position would hold far too much responsibility.

'It would stress me out far too much to drive through London. No,' she held out a hand, 'the matter's settled and not up for negotiation.'

'Well I'm sorry, Diana, I can't do it.

There are too many calls on my time as it is, and I'm a journalist not a chauffeur,' Abbie said firmly anxious to make a stand in the face of Diana's high handedness.

The same sly look that occasionally crept into Molly's eyes crept into Diana's. 'Talking of your article, didn't you originally want an exclusive from me?'

'Yes and I still hope to get it.'

'I absolutely refuse to be interviewed by you.' Diana tilted her chin in challenge.

'But you promised,' Abbie retaliated, outraged at this blatant display of unprofessionalism.

'I could of course be persuaded to change my mind.' Diana licked her peachy pink lips, a light of triumph in her eyes. She had won and she knew it.

Abbie had quite simply been out manoeuvred.

'Actually, Abbie it is quite a good idea,' Sim said, agreeing with his mother.

'When I need your help I'll ask for it,'

she turned on him.

He ignored her outburst. 'There are far too many interruptions at Waterside Cottage but just think, there'd only be the two of you in the car and the journey to the studio takes over two hours. You could get through a lot of copy in that time.'

Sim did have a point.

'Do I have your permission to use my tape recorder?' Abbie asked.

'Yes, yes,' now she had won, Diana was prepared to be magnanimous, 'Sim's my witness. You have my full permission to use whatever aids you like. What other endorsement do you need?'

'Nothing,' Abbie said muttering, 'thanks a bunch,' under her breath to Sim.

'Don't grind your teeth, darling,' Diana frowned at her, 'it's such an unattractive habit. It quite ages you. Now,' she clapped her hands, 'have you made your new appointment with me, Sim?'

'Yes, for Thursday and I've written it down. Look.'

Diana waved away his attempt to tell her the details. 'You have? Good. Then I suggest we have a nightcap and you tell me exactly what went on at this party of Molly's. I may stroll down to The Jolly Molly in the morning. It's time my mother stopped sulking and came home, don't you think?'

Orla Faces Up To The Past

'Do you have any close relations, Ms Dillaine?' The doctor looked up from reading his notes.

'My father passed away last winter. I have two brothers and several nephews,' Orla replied, 'but no one else.'

'I see.' He glanced down again at her medical records. 'Have you ever married?'

'Just once. A long time ago.' Orla felt a nervous flutter in her chest. She suspected what was coming next.

Dr Jones hesitated before saying, 'You gave birth to a child twenty-five years ago?'

Orla bit her lip. 'Yes. I had a baby — a daughter. It was when I lived in England.'

'I see, and where is the child now?'

'Her father left me, so she was put up for adoption. A friend of mine arranged it through the church.'

'Has there been any contact between you and your daughter since?'

'No.' Orla's voice was hoarse. She still found it difficult to talk about the baby she had lost. There were very few people who even knew she had had a child and Orla liked to keep it that way.

'And she has never tried to find you?'

'She has not.'

'Are you in touch with the father of the child? I only ask because maybe she has been in touch with him?'

'He's dead,' Orla said quietly.

'I see.' Doctor Jones capped his pen and smiled professionally at her. 'Well you are in remarkably good health, Ms Dillaine, but I would suggest your brothers and their families get themselves tested. It's a relatively easy thing to do and there is no cause for concern but the sooner we spot these things the better.'

Orla caught her breath. She had put

her recent spells of tiredness and lack of energy down to overwork. Her bookings were up over fifty per cent this year and the extra business had entailed a lot of work and it was not unusual for Orla to work an eighteen hour day.

This had been her first chance to get herself a medical check up and what the doctor had told her had totally turned her world upside down.

'I'm not ill am I?' Orla could feel the rapid beating of her heart in her chest.

Doctor Jones shook his head. 'There's nothing to worry about at all. Your type of diabetes is very mild and easily controlled by diet these days so there's no need for injections or any special treatment, but it is a condition that tends to run in families, so that is why I would suggest you mention it to your brothers and their children. Now I'll make another appointment for you to have a check up in six months' time and I'll ask my receptionist to sort out some leaflets for you to read. The condition needs regular monitoring just to be on the safe side.'

'Would my daughter inherit this condition too, Doctor Jones?' Orla asked.

'Your type of diabetes tends to manifest itself in older patients,' Doctor Jones replied.

'But it is possible?'

'Yes, it's possible,' he admitted.

★ ★ ★

Orla took the coast road back to her studio. It was a drive she usually enjoyed and it never failed to lift her spirits, but today she didn't have eyes for the backdrop scenery or the heart to appreciate the startling blue of the ocean. Today she could only think about what the doctor had told her.

It would be easy to get in touch with her two brothers and their families. She would motor up at the weekend. It had been a while since she had seen them and they were due a visit. That just left Caitlin — Abbie, Johnny had called her.

If as Johnny suspected, Abbie Rogers was Orla's daughter, then she had a right to know this latest piece of news. As her birth mother it was the least Orla could do for her. But if she wasn't Abbie's mother, Orla bit her lip. She realised she could be stirring up a whole nest of trouble.

Orla tried to remember exactly what Johnny had told her about Abbie. He thought she had grown up in Devon. It was an area of England Orla knew little about. Apart from the farmhouse break she had enjoyed with Barney and Diana and Don, due to sickness on the set, she had never visited the county. Her time had been spent mainly in London, or at Diana's house in Surrey.

It was possible for her daughter to have grown up in Devon she supposed and it would be an ironic coincidence. Her forty-eight hour enforced farmhouse break there had been a magical time and one she would cherish forever.

The church had arranged the adoption but Orla presumed the records would be confidential so there would be no way she could check the details. The identity of all parties would be kept a secret from each other. It had been one of their most stringent rules.

If a child was to start a new life with new parents, then those new parents had to be confident that a tearful mother who might be having second thoughts about keeping her baby would not snatch their baby away from them.

Orla had been made to read the paperwork so many times she still almost knew it off by heart.

The photograph Johnny had emailed her showed a girl who shared Orla's hair colour and pale skin. There was nothing unusual in that, but there was the brooch — a five-pointed star with diamonds. It had been the only thing Orla had been able to give her daughter — a present from Diana, before they fell out.

When babies were handed over to their adoptive families, their birth mothers were not allowed to give them any gifts, but Orla had managed to pin the brooch into the folds of the shawl her baby had been wearing.

It had been a gesture of defiance and love. Orla was prepared to break the strict rules to let her child know she loved her and using the brooch had been the only way she could demonstrate that love.

Orla turned her car into the forecourt of her studio. Party balloons were still tied to the gates and bounced gently against each other in the midday breeze. One of the youngsters had celebrated their eighteenth birthday two nights ago and Orla had allowed her and her friends to use the studio to celebrate, on the understanding the party was not posted on the net and that the guest list was closely controlled.

Several responsible adults were also in attendance. Her precautions had been a wise move and the party had passed off without any unpleasant incidents.

She got out of the car and carefully undid the balloons, puncturing them and placing them in one of the large rubbish bins that were in constant use at the studio.

Her daughter would be twenty-five years old now. Had she had an eighteenth birthday party? Orla would never know. There was so much of her life she would have missed. The first day at school, her exam successes, boyfriends, all the usual things a daughter shared with her mother, how Orla wished she could have shared them with Caitlin.

She walked slowly up the steps and into the sun filled studio. It was Friday afternoon and the college students always left early for the holiday weekend. Normally Orla would take a trip out in the currach, perhaps visit the next bay, do a little sketching or write a poem to de-stress, but not today.

The germ of an idea was slowly beginning to take seed in her mind. The one thing she did know about her daughter was her date of birth. Every midsummer's day she lit a candle and every midsummer's day at exactly half-past-two in the afternoon she stopped whatever she was doing for a few moment's quiet reflection.

If Johnny could find out Abbie Rogers' date of birth and it turned out to be midsummer's day, Orla decided she would go to England. She would visit Diana. So what if they hadn't spoken to each other for over twenty-five years? Her daughter's health was far more important than old grievances and misunderstandings.

She flipped open her laptop and began typing in Johnny's email address.

Abbie Hears A Startling Revelation

'Dear girl, I am so sorry you were roped into all this madness. Whatever must you think?'

'Johnny?' Abbie looked up from trying to make some sense of her scribbled notes. Diana had talked nineteen to the dozen on the drive up and Abbie wanted to write everything down while it was still fresh in her memory. She had the tape as back up, but sometimes recordings of interviews were garbled because the tape became twisted or split. 'What are you doing here? I thought you were still in Ireland.'

'Only got back late last night. The weather was fine so I stayed over longer than I intended then my flight was delayed by some air traffic control bother. I'm sorry I missed Molly's party. I had intended to be there. Did you have a good time? You did go, I presume?'

'It was an experience,' Abbie admitted, trying not to remember holding hands with Sim on the walk home.

That must have been a moment's madness she had decided as she struggled to get to sleep in the small hours, and one she definitely would not be repeating.

'Molly's parties normally are a bit alternative. Glad she managed to keep it a secret from you, even if she did have to manufacture a row with Dee to make extra sure. Dee cannot keep a secret to save her life so it was vital she didn't find out about the party until the actual night in question. Are the pair of them talking again now?'

'Think so.'

Abbie was having difficulty getting her head round the complicated arrangements that had been made to keep her party a secret. Just when she thought she had got the sum of the Foxton family, they were wrong footed by doing something so incredibly unexpected it took her breath away.

'What's that you're drinking?' Johnny asked.

'Coffee. Want some?'

'No thanks. I'm awash with the stuff.' Johnny sat down opposite her. 'So, what's been going on while I've been away apart from the party?'

'Theo and I have made a start on the photos for Diana's book and Diana's been booked for speeding again.'

Johnny made a face. 'I know and you shouldn't have let Dee talk you into chauffeuring her around. It's an abuse of your time.'

'I couldn't really get out of it.' Privately Abbie agreed with him. She still felt annoyed with herself for having been talked into acting as Diana's temporary driver, but there was nothing she could do about it now. 'Like I said, she was caught speeding for the third time and she's scared she's going to lose her licence.'

'That's as may be, but Dee is perfectly capable of looking after herself. She just likes to use people.'

'She has promised me an exclusive interview for my article. You remember the one I'm doing on actresses of the seventies if I drove her up today for her voice-over and management meetings? I agreed. I can't afford to turn down any offer like that.'

'It wasn't necessary.'

'Johnny, it was. I don't care if you have a problem with my actions, but my job at Waterside Cottage won't last forever. When it finishes I need to get a life and for that I also need money. The article will provide me with significant funding.'

Johnny waved away Abbie's explanation. 'That's as may be, but I bet one thing Dee didn't tell you was that the agents offered her a car and driver for this job today?'

Abbie's jaw dropped.

'No, she didn't.'

'I thought not. Dee all over, that is. Well, I'm the commissioned driver and that's why I'm here today. I couldn't believe it when I turned up at Waterside Cottage to collect Dee. Molly told me what had happened. I must have only missed you by about ten minutes. I virtually followed you all the way up here. Blasted woman. I nearly got caught speeding myself. And you know what? If we confront her about all this she'll put it down to forgetfulness or some such nonsense and she'll get away with it. She always does.'

Nothing would have surprised Abbie about the Foxtons any more. They were a law unto themselves.

'Well, we can't do anything about it now,' she said, 'it's a done deal and Diana did actually give me some useful information about an envelope full of old theatre programmes Theo and I discovered tucked away in the back of the photo album. I brought it along with me today to look at while I was waiting for her to do her voice-over.

189

Did you know Diana used to be on the stage before she got the part in *Masquerade*?'

A shadow crossed Johnny's face. 'Actually, Abbie,' he hesitated, 'you don't want to hang around here all day do you? I mean I'm sure you've better things to do.'

'I have but I can't just leave.'

'Dee will be here for hours. Fancy some lunch? I know it's a bit early but there's a good place down the road. It'll take us about half an hour's gentle stroll to get there. What do you say? We can leave a note at reception telling them where we've gone and you needn't worry about driving Dee home. I may as well earn my very generous fee. I'll bring her back.'

Abbie glanced out to the garden surrounding the studio. It was in an area of north London she didn't really know but she had been thinking about taking a walk to get a breath of fresh air after the long drive from Surrey.

'Fine.' She picked up her bag. 'Give

me a few moments to freshen up and I'll be with you.'

* * *

The good place Johnny knew down the road turned out to be run by an old friend of his, and Henri let them sit outside in his private garden while he prepared his signature fish bouillabaisse.

'It will make your senses cry,' he said as he put his fingers to his lips and kissed them. 'Half an hour?'

'Great chap, Henri,' Johnny said as they settled themselves in a couple of easy chairs. 'We used to work together in Hong Kong. He ran a restaurant out there.'

Abbie had never really enquired as to what Johnny did for a living. His working life seemed to have ranged from playing bit parts in the theatre and television, to long spells abroad.

'No idea,' Theo had answered Abbie's question when she had asked him about

191

Johnny's career. 'All I can tell you is that he and Diana go way back.'

'Did you have a good holiday?' Abbie asked.

'Wonderful. Do you know Dingle Bay at all?'

'I've never been to Ireland. I've always wanted to go.'

'The peninsula is a beautiful area. The views are breathtaking. I played a little golf and caught up with some old friends, one old friend in particular.' He cleared his throat and looked away from Abbie.

'Yes?' she coaxed.

'She runs a studio workshop place in a tiny fishing hamlet on the peninsula, designing Celtic jewellery, that sort of thing.'

'Very nice,' Abbie smiled at him. 'Is she an old flame?'

'Good lord, no. Nothing like that.' Johnny coloured up. 'Her name's Orla Dillaine.'

'I've heard of her,' Abbie frowned. Why did that name keep cropping up?

'Isn't she in one of those old photographs of Diana's?'

'More than one I expect. At one time they were very close. She used to look after Dee's wardrobe.'

'Of course.' Abbie's brow cleared. 'She's the one with the red hair isn't she? The one everyone keeps saying looks like me. I think I asked Diana about her but she wasn't very forthcoming.'

'She wouldn't have been. They had a spectacular falling out.'

'Everyone falls out with Diana some time or another, but it doesn't mean anything.'

'This row was a lot more serious than one of Dee's usual spats. This one involved her husband — Don Foxton I mean, Theo and Sim's father.'

'What happened between them?'

'It's not really my place to say. Orla and I remained friends over the years although we don't see each other as often as we'd like to.'

'I see.'

'And was she well?'

'Yes. Yes.' Johnny looked out over the lawn with a distracted look on his face, as if he hadn't heard Abbie's polite question.

'Tell me, did you know Diana's second husband? Barney, wasn't it? Nobody seems to mention him much.'

'He died too,' Johnny said after a pause. 'He was a cameraman.'

'What happened to him?'

'It was all a bit sad. He was driving home from work and on the way he picked up Theo's wife, Bethan's mother. She'd been doing a bit of shopping or something.'

The atmosphere in the garden had grown very still. Abbie hardly dared move. The sun was warm on the bare flesh of her arm, but she fought down an urge to shiver. 'There was a fatal accident. No one really knew what happened. The car ran off the road. No other vehicle was involved. It was a fine evening and there was nothing wrong with the car.'

'Do you think they were having an argument?'

'I don't think so. They hardly knew each other. They think Barney might have fallen asleep at the wheel. He'd been working a long day. The coroner brought in a verdict of accidental death.'

'I don't remember reading anything about it in the newspapers.'

'It was general election night so there was a lot of other news going on at the time, the family managed to hush it up.'

'How sad for them,' Abbie said in a soft voice.

'Bethan was only a baby at the time so Dee took her in and Theo sold his house. He said he couldn't bear to live there without Cathy. He's lived at Waterside Cottage on and off ever since.'

'You would like to eat outside?' Henri appeared on the terrace. 'It is a lovely day and I know the English, they like to eat in the garden, where they are attacked by wasps and eating disgusting soggy sandwiches.'

'There's no need to exaggerate,' Johnny's smile was back in place as he greeted his old friend. 'Eating outside is one of the great pleasures of life and yes, we'd like to have lunch out here?' He raised his eyebrows at Abbie. 'If that's all right with you?'

A few moments later two steaming bowls of Henri's celebrated fish soup were placed in front of them, along with hunks of fresh bread.

'Today I have put in my very best langoustines, with some monkfish and crab. That piquant smell is the finest herbs and the orange peel. I do not expect to find any soup left in the bowls when I return to clear the table otherwise war will be declared. Bon appétit.'

'Better do as he says,' Johnny handed over the breadbasket, 'otherwise I'll never be able to show my face here again.'

Abbie nibbled at a crust of bread as thoughts crowded into her mind.

'By the way you have my assurance I wouldn't have any such personal information in my piece on Diana,' she informed Johnny. 'It would be intrusive, especially as it's not general knowledge and I really intend my article to focus on her career.'

'I didn't doubt your integrity for one moment,' Johnny replied. 'Now for goodness sake eat some of that soup, and stop filling yourself up with bread.'

Abbie picked up her spoon and did as Johnny bid her. 'It's delicious,' she said through a mouthful of hot langoustine. 'Mm. I can taste the fresh herbs.'

'Tell you what, we've had enough talk about old scandals, why don't you talk about your family while we eat? Didn't you once tell me you came from Devon?'

'Yes. We lived by the sea. My father was a vicar.'

'Did you have any brothers or sisters?'

'No. I was an only child.'

'Weren't you lonely?'

'There's always so much going on in a vicarage you don't get time to be lonely.'

'I had a wonderful holiday in Devon once.' Johnny began recounting another of his tales, 'with some sailing chums of mine. We took this boat out and there was the most tremendous storm. I've never forgotten it. Quite put me off sailing ever since. I don't even like going on Molly's little tub. It brings it all back.'

Johnny gossiped on about his holiday and his friends and when Abbie put down her spoon a few minutes later she was surprised to realise she had finished her bowl of soup.

'Good girl,' Johnny said. 'Knew my diversion tactics would work. Henri will be pleased. Want some dessert? Fruit flan?'

'I couldn't manage a thing.' Abbie held up a hand in defeat.

'Ah, here's Henri. 'Fraid our little friend can't eat any more. I'll have some of your cheese, I think.'

Beaming with pleasure at the sight of the empty bowls Henri bustled away.

'So,' Abbie prompted, 'what else did you do in Ireland?'

Johnny cut himself a chunk of cheese before replying. 'Perhaps you should know,' he said, ignoring her question, 'that the reason Dee never mentions Orla is because the rumour was she had an affair with Don Foxton.'

'Theo mentioned something of the sort when we were going through Diana's photographs, but he was only a child at the time so he didn't know any of the details.'

'There weren't any. Orla denied it, but Dee didn't believe her. Next thing any of us knew Orla had upped and offed back to Ireland. Dee was distraught. She and Orla had been so very close you see. I was the only one who kept in touch with her.'

'What a sad story.'

'I couldn't mention my suspicions to Dee, because it would have raked up all the old memories, and of course there was always the possibility that I might have got it wrong.'

Abbie blinked. 'Got what wrong?' she asked in confusion. Had she missed something Johnny had said?

'I mean there are lots of them, aren't there?'

'Lots of what?'

'Brooches. You remember that photo we took? The day we had lunch to celebrate Theo's homecoming?' Abbie nodded. 'Well I sent a copy across to Orla. It was the brooch you see. I thought if Orla saw the resemblance . . .'

'The brooch?' Abbie's heartbeat quickened.

'The one you showed Bethan? The one you say you can't find? Please, Abbie,' Johnny put a hand over hers, 'I'm not prying but you told Bethan your mother gave it to you?'

'Yes.' Abbie nodded.

'Is it a diamond and ruby star?'

'Yes.'

'And where did you really get it?'

'I found it among my father's things. There was an old cashbox in his desk and I suppose he must have locked it away and forgotten all about it. He wasn't very worldly you see and it would never have occurred to him it ought to have been insured.'

'Why were you looking at it the night you arrived at Waterside Cottage?'

Abbie took a deep breath. 'Because when I discovered it, it was wrapped up in a piece of notepaper headed *Diana LaTrobe*.'

Underneath his outdoor tan, Johnny's skin had turned pale. He listened intently as Abbie continued. 'The note said 'for the baby'.'

'And you think the baby was you?'

'Who else could it be?' Abbie demanded. 'My father didn't move in Diana's circles. I don't think he ever went to the cinema and he never watched *Masquerade* on the television. He wouldn't know who Diana LaTrobe was.'

'And your mother?' Johnny asked softly. 'Would she have known Diana?'

Abbie shook her head. 'I actually don't know who my real mother is or my father come to that. You see, I'm adopted.'

'In that case, Abbie,' Johnny began, 'there's something you should know.'

'You're trying to tell me Diana is my mother, aren't you?'

'No, I'm not.'

'Why else would she part with such a valuable piece of jewellery?'

'You've got it all wrong, Abbie. Dee isn't your mother.'

'Then what is it you've got to tell me?'

Johnny took a deep breath. 'If the rumours are to be believed then Don Foxton was your father.'

'What?'

'I know this will come as a bit of a shock to you, but . . . '

'That means,' Abbie could barely get the words out, 'that Sim and Theo Foxton are my brothers.'

'I'm Leaving Waterside Cottage Now'

'Thank heavens you're back.' Sim was waiting for Abbie at the front door of Waterside Cottage. 'Johnny's been on the telephone several times. He said you left him hours ago. He's been frantic with worry. Where've you been?'

'There was no need to keep tabs on me,' Abbie retorted. 'I stopped off on the way to check on the availability of a flat I'd seen advertised in the paper.'

Sim frowned. 'I don't understand. I thought you were staying here until you'd completed your interview with Diana.'

'No. I'm leaving Waterside Cottage now, tonight.'

'What are you talking about? Have you had an argument with Diana?'

'It's quite simple,' Abbie brushed Sim

203

aside. 'Will you let me pass please? I have to do my packing.'

'No I will not,' he objected. 'Look, we haven't got time for all this now. We've got an emergency on our hands. I need the car. Molly's gone to the hospital.'

'What?' Abbie shrieked. 'What's happened?'

'She went in the ambulance with Bethan.'

'Has she had an accident on her bike?'

'No, on her horse.'

'Molly's been riding a horse?' Abbie repeated in a daze.

'Abbie, stop talking nonsense and listen. Are you sure you're feeling all right?'

'Tell me what's happened,' she repeated.

'I need your help.' Sim spoke slowly and carefully. 'Molly asked me to pack a few of her things but I don't know the sort of stuff a female needs for an overnight stay. Can you do it?'

'A nightie and some toiletries, but tell

me is she badly hurt?'

The thought of Molly lying injured in the road was almost too much to bear.

'They think she's broken her arm. Where are you going?' he asked as Abbie turned to leave the house.

'To the Jolly Molly to pick up Molly's stuff.'

'What is the matter with you, Abbie? Aren't you listening to a word I've said? We're talking about Bethan, not Molly.'

'Bethan?'

'She went for a ride after school and the pony lost its footing down a rabbit hole. Bethan fell off. Luckily a neighbour spotted what happened and managed to get hold of Molly immediately. She contacted me too because Theo's away on business. He borrowed my car so I'm temporarily without transport. You had Diana's car — but never mind all that,' Sim frowned, 'what was all that about leaving?' Sim demanded. 'You can't leave. We need you here.' He grabbed her hand.

'No,' Abbie backed off. 'You mustn't

touch me.' She batted his hand away.

'Now what's wrong?'

'Just keep your distance.'

'If this is about Susannah?' Sim began.

'It isn't and I have to get Bethan's things.' Abbie was pleased to have a reason to rush away from Sim. She didn't want to think about what had so nearly happened between them. Right now Bethan was injured and she was Abbie's top priority. Everything else would have to be put on hold.

Grabbing a sponge bag she put in toothpaste and a flannel. She flung a few more essentials into an overnight bag then raced back down the stairs.

'I'm ready,' she gasped. 'You drive. I don't know the way.'

'Get in,' Sim ordered, his face a controlled mask of confusion.

*　*　*

The hospital was only a few miles outside the village of Hamwater but never had a drive seemed so long to Abbie. Conversation between her and Sim was restricted to a few clipped sentences as they battled their way through the evening rush hour.

'Blasted market day,' Sim said, pressing down hard on the horn. 'Get a move on,' he bellowed at the driver in front when he didn't immediately respond to the traffic lights, as they turned from red to green.

'Calm down, Sim,' Abbie implored him. 'We don't want another accident or any more tickets for speeding.'

'We have to get to Bethan.'

'I'm sure Molly can be relied upon to do everything that's necessary. Drive to arrive,' she insisted as they narrowly missed colliding with a bollard.

'Sorry,' Sim apologised. 'You're right. I'm not thinking straight. When you didn't arrived back on time I began to imagine something had happened to you as well.' He slid a hand over hers and squeezed her fingers.

Abbie gritted her teeth. If she

snatched her hand away now, they might well have an accident Sim was so tensed up. She looked out of the window and breathed a silent sigh of relief as Sim put his hand back on the steering wheel.

'Tell me about your day,' he said. 'It might help to calm me down. Trust Theo to be out of town when something like this happens. Have you had a row with Diana? Is that why you want to leave?'

Abbie shook her head. 'No, it's nothing like that.'

'What then?' Sim was now gripping the steering wheel so tightly his knuckles protruded. He half turned his face to look at Abbie. 'If it's not about Diana and it's not about Susannah, is it something I've done?' A shadow crossed his face. 'If it's Theo up to his old tricks,' Sim paused. 'Abbie what's the matter? Tell me. You've gone deathly pale.'

'Can we talk about something else?' Abbie implored.

'Only if you promise to tell me what it's all about later.'

'I will.'

Abbie wasn't sure she would be around to talk to Sim later but it was the only reassurance she could give him at the moment.

'Is it anything to do with Johnny?'

'I said leave it,' Abbie snapped. 'Sorry,' she apologised, 'it's not your fault. I'm a bit tense.'

'Aren't we all? None of this would have happened if Diana hadn't forgotten Johnny was her driver for the day. Seems he'd rushed back from his holiday especially. The flight was delayed then he arrived at Waterside Cottage to find Diana had left without him. It's not Johnny who has upset you is it?' Sim asked. 'He can be a bit insensitive at times and according to Molly he was pretty angry when he drove off after you. He hasn't been taking it out on you has he?'

'No, it's nothing he's done.'

Abbie wished Sim would concentrate

on the road and leave her to her thoughts. There had been so many shocks over the past few days she wasn't sure what to think about anything any more.

'Here we are.' Sim braked to a halt outside the Accident and Emergency department of the local hospital. 'You go inside and see if you can find out what's happening while I park the car.'

★ ★ ★

'Lady LaTrobe?' Abbie burst through the doors to reception and accosted the nurse. 'She came in with her granddaughter, Bethan Foxton — a suspected broken arm?'

'Take a seat,' the duty nurse indicated a blue plastic chair in the waiting area.

'Is Bethan all right?' Abbie demanded.

'She's in X-ray now. As soon as I hear anything I'll let you know.'

Abbie sat down and looked round. She hated hospitals. Ever since breaking her own arm as a child after falling

210

down the stairs. The antiseptic smell brought back memories she would rather forget.

She looked down at the pathetic little overnight bag she was carrying. Bethan was the sweetest child in the world and surprisingly mature for her age. She was always on hand with cups of tea and toasted sandwiches for supper when there was nothing but some cheese in the fridge. They'd giggled their way through all the episodes of *Masquerade* now, laughing at the fashions and the hair. It was Bethan's birthday next week and Abbie had promised her a trip to a nail bar.

'My first grown up treat,' Bethan had said excitedly.

Now it looked like everything was off.

Abbie looked round the stark waiting area. If Bethan didn't want to stay overnight, Abbie would move heaven and earth to make sure she was allowed home. Between them they could set up a nursing roster. She would need love and care and a bit of special attention and Abbie would make sure she got it. She leaned back and closed her eyes. The drive back from north London had been long and stressful and her head ached.

Sim strode through the sliding doors. 'Any news?' His voice jolted Abbie's eyes open.

'She's in X-ray.'

He sat down beside her. 'I suppose I ought to contact Theo but they don't let you use mobile phones in hospital do they?'

'There's a pay phone on the wall.' Abbie nodded to a booth in the corner. 'Try that.'

Sim was back moments later.

'Did you get through?' Abbie asked.

'Yes. I rang his mobile. Susannah answered.'

'What?' Abbie raised voice drew a startled look from the nurse on the desk.

'It seems he took Susannah along with him as a companion while he conducted his business.' Sim held up a hand. 'Don't say anything, Abbie. It's a situation we've been through before. The important thing is he knows about Bethan and he'll be making his way back home as soon as he can. How much longer have we got to wait?' he demanded. 'Surely it can't take that long to work out if the bone's broken or not?'

'Are you the child's next of kin?' the nurse asked as Sim strode over to the desk.

'No. I'm her uncle.'

'Then as I explained to your companion,' the nurse said firmly, 'there is no news at the moment.'

'Want some coffee?' Sim demanded.

'Let's find a machine,' Abbie said softly, putting a hand under his elbow and drawing him away from the desk. Her confused mind was beginning to register the fact that Bethan could also be her niece as well. 'It won't do our cause any good by upsetting the staff.'

'Her little face was so pale, but all she

could think about was Paddy.' Sim's voice caught in his throat.

'They aren't going to put him down?' Abbie asked. 'He didn't break a bone too?'

'No, he's fine. He recovered himself. They're looking after him at the stable. It's Bethan I'm worried about. She's such a brave child. Not a bit like the rest of us. I don't know how she puts up with us all.'

'Then the best thing we can do is to be strong for her now she needs us, wouldn't you say?' Abbie asked softly pushing personal issues aside.

The look Sim gave Abbie almost melted her resolve not to touch him, but apart from their brief contact when she'd dragged him away from the enquiry desk, Abbie had kept firmly to her resolution to avoid physical contact.

'Look, isn't that a drinks' dispenser?' Abbie asked.

Abbie presumed the liquid she was drinking was a cup of tea. It didn't taste like any tea she'd ever had before, but it eased the dryness scorching her throat. Her head buzzed from the fatigue caused by the early start to the day when she and Diana had driven through the London rush hour and then Johnny arriving out of the blue and delivering his lunchtime shock to end all shocks — and now this.

'Abbie.'

She jumped at the sound of her name.

'What?'

'You didn't mean what you said about leaving us, did you? You will stay and help look after Bethan won't you? I mean she's going to need intensive nursing. Diana's very flaky when it comes to that sort of thing and I'm not entirely sure I trust Molly to be reliable.'

'I — let's see what the doctors say.'

'What is it, Abbie?' Sim implored. 'What's gone wrong between us? I know you don't want to talk about it now, but was it what I said down by the river last night? Did I come on too strong?'

Abbie wasn't too sure she could remember exactly what Sim had said but all she could remember was if he had wanted to kiss her she wouldn't have stopped him. She now knew that was a situation that must never arise again. Theo too must be discouraged from touching her.

'You can see Susannah and I have a very casual relationship,' Sim's lips tightened. 'So casual she's gone away with Theo, so there's no need to worry on her account.'

'No, Sim. It's nothing to do with any of that.' Abbie forced herself to smile at him. 'If I promise to stay on and help nurse Abbie, will you do something for me in return?'

'Anything,' Sim said eagerly.

Will you promise not to be alone with me again?'

'Why?'

'Or Theo?'

'Let me get this straight,' Sim said, his face an expression of confusion. 'You don't want me or Theo to be alone in the same room as you again?'

'Yes.'

'No, I can't possibly promise that, Abbie.'

'You have to.'

'Has Theo said or done something to upset you?'

'No.'

'Have I?'

'No.'

'Then what possible reason can you have for not wanting us to be alone with you?'

'I can't explain, but I can't possibly nurse Bethan unless you agree.'

The expression on Sim's face was in danger of now turning into a snarl. 'Is my presence in the same room as you really so repugnant? No, don't answer that. I can see the truth from the expression in your eyes. Very well. I'll do as you say.' He stood up. 'There's Molly.' He waved across to his grandmother. 'But I'm not telling Theo for you. You'll have to do your own dirty work and tell him yourself.'

Abbie Remains At Waterside Cottage

'I'm bored already, Molly,' Bethan flopped down on the sofa letting out a huge sigh.

'Only boring people are bored,' Molly looked up from reading her motorbike magazine, 'surely you know that, my pet?'

'My arm hurts,' she whined, 'and I keep wanting to scratch it and I can't.'

'It'll get better soon.' Molly did her best to soothe the fractious child.

'And why hasn't Uncle Sim been to visit?' Bethan pouted. 'He hasn't been in all week.' Her lower lip stuck out even further.

'He's very busy at the moment, darling, and so is Daddy with his new project.'

Molly cast a speculative glance at

Abbie who was seated at her desk studiously updating her database file.

'Isn't that so, Abbie?'

'Yes, very busy.' Abbie did her best to sound upbeat but ever since her confrontation with Sim being positive hadn't been easy. Bethan had taken to being difficult due to her enforced inactivity and not being allowed to visit Paddy. Diana who hated not being the centre of attention had also started to play up, insisting on frequent updates on Abbie's work and demanding to know what she paid her for if there was no progress.

The situation at Waterside Cottage resembled a ticking time bomb long overdue for an explosion.

'There you are then,' Molly's weather-beaten face creased into a smile. 'Abbie agrees with me. Everyone's very busy and it's time you learned that the world does not revolve around you, young Bethan.'

'It's no good asking Abbie anything these days,' Bethan grumbled. 'She doesn't smile or laugh any more.'

'Neither do you. Where's my Miss Sunshine?' Molly attempted to cheer her up. 'It's not like you to be so long in the face.'

'I'm bored,' Bethan repeated, kicking her foot aimlessly backwards and forwards. 'I can't ride Paddy. All my friends are at school. I've watched all my DVDs and Abbie's on the computer so I can't play my new game. I can't anyway with my arm in a sling. What can I do?' she wailed.

'Why don't we got for a walk?' Molly suggested brightly, 'down to The Jolly Molly? You like it down by the river. We could feed the ducks and there are a few things I need to see to on board. I know, let's take the dogs. They need the exercise, and so do you.' Molly frowned at Bethan. 'That's why you're being so grumpy — lack of exercise.'

'All right,' Bethan perked up a little and jumped to her feet. 'Would you like to come as well, Abbie? Perhaps it would stop you from being grumpy too.'

'I need to work on my notes,' Abbie said, casting a shamefaced smile at Bethan. The child was right. She did need something to lift her spirits but she didn't think a walk down to the river would do the trick. 'I'm only looking grumpy because I'm concentrating and let me tell you, it's not easy with you mooning about the place and interrupting me all the time with a face that would turn milk sour. Where's my lovely smiling Bethan gone?'

'She's here really,' Bethan assured her, 'you do still love me, don't you?' she asked anxiously.

'Come here.' Abbie held out her arms and the child ran into them. Abbie hugged her, careful to avoid hurting her fractured arm. 'There, friends again?'

'Friends.' Bethan's little face looked happier than when she'd stomped into the room a few moments ago.

The fracture was not as serious as had at first been feared but the doctors had advised Molly and Diana to keep Bethan off school for a few days while things settled down.

'Right then off you go with Molly and have a nice time.'

As Bethan ran from the room to fetch a jumper, Molly walked across to Abbie.

'I know it's none of my business,' she began, 'but have you and Sim had a falling out?'

'Of course not.' Abbie returned her attention to her work as Molly loomed over her.

'Then would you please pay me the courtesy of looking at me while I'm speaking to you?' Molly said in a tone of voice she hadn't used on Abbie before.

Abbie flushed realising her response had bordered on rudeness and that Molly had every right to take her to task.

'Sorry,' she apologised. 'I've got a lot on my mind.'

'Apology accepted.' Molly waited a

few moments before saying, 'I'm glad you've made things up with Bethan,' Molly said, 'because whatever is going on here is nothing to do with the child is it? And it's not fair to take it out on her.'

Although Molly did not raise her voice, her words held all the strength of a whiplash.

'Nothing is going on,' Abbie insisted.

'I don't like to see my great granddaughter upset, neither do I like to see the people I care about most in the world, tiptoeing around each other as if they were walking on eggshells. I can accept Diana's displays of temperament, it's in her blood, but I do not accept them from you. Now, what's with the long face? Come on, confession is good for the soul.'

'It's nothing, really I've been trying to get my head round these scribbled notes I made about Diana for days now and without Theo's input it's a bit tricky, that's all.'

'Then you've only yourself to blame.'

Molly's voice held no sympathy. 'You're as prickly as a hedgehog these days. It's no wonder neither of my grandsons is on speaking terms with you at the moment. May I ask if either of them has upset you?'

'No.' Abbie repeated, wishing Molly would let the subject drop. She was far too astute to be fooled by any story Abbie could invent as to why she and Sim were no longer the friends they once were.

'Then is it me or Diana? Have we done something wrong?'

'You know you haven't.'

'So what exactly is going on?' Molly persisted with her enquiries. 'And don't tell me nothing because I won't believe you. You could have cut the atmosphere with a knife on the drive home from the hospital last week. Sim hasn't been near Waterside Cottage since and Theo's taken himself off again. Even Diana's noticed something isn't right and it takes a lot to get through to her. I'm pretty sure the boys haven't fallen out with each other, so that leaves you.'

'And Susannah?' Abbie suggested. She knew she was clutching at straws but she had to get Molly off her back before she stumbled on the truth. 'When Sim telephoned Theo's mobile from the hospital, Susannah answered.'

'Rubbish.' Molly dismissed that one with all the contempt it deserved. 'My boys have got more sense than to fall out with each other over Susannah Green and even if they had, Susannah is nothing to do with you. So that still doesn't explain why you and Sim are at loggerheads.'

'I'm ready.' Bethan bounded back into the room, her face no longer sulky.

'Off we go then, darling,' Molly smiled at her great granddaughter. 'You'd better find the dog leads. We don't want anyone falling in the water. I'll be with you in five minutes.' She turned back to Abbie. 'And what's all this about you looking for a flat? The agency was on the phone again this morning. I took the call. I didn't have a clue what they were talking about. Bethan enlightened me. She's very upset you know. She thinks she's done something wrong.'

'I was thinking of moving out.' Abbie didn't think it was possible to feel more wretched than she already did, but Molly wasn't pulling any punches.

'Why? Isn't there enough room here for you?'

Abbie all but squirmed in her chair. This was worse than being in trouble at school.

'I really do need to get my article on Diana finished and there are too many interruptions at Waterside Cottage.'

Even to her own ears Abbie knew her explanation sounded lame.

'Hogwash,' Molly retaliated. 'You could shut yourself away in no end of places. There's the old boathouse you could use, or your room, or you could take yourself off to the local library. None of the Foxtons ever goes there.'

'Molly,' Abbie ran out of excuses as she looked into the kindly, concerned face. 'I have got something on my mind but I can't tell you about it,' she admitted, 'I've thought things through and it's best that I leave Waterside Cottage.'

'Very well. I realise I can't stop you leaving,' Molly said with quiet dignity, 'but I can tell you I don't want you to go. You are as dear to me as my own family, but I also realise your private life is your own affair and that I have no right to pry. Despite what you say, my instinct tells me you need help but you're probably too proud to ask for it. If you don't want to tell me about it then I won't press you, but I want you to know if you are in trouble you can confide in me. You may feel like deserting us, but I will never desert you. That's all I have to say on the matter. Bethan and I are going out.'

Feeling as if she had been stabbed through the heart, Abbie watched Molly leave the room. How had it come to this? She had hurt the one person in the world she loved as much as her own parents.

Dear Molly who had shown her nothing but kindness. If Abbie had been the type of girl who cried, she would put her head down on the table and sobbed her heart out. As it was she sat at her desk battling to control the huge lump blocking her throat.

'Bye, Abbie.' She heard Bethan's excited voice in the corridor outside trying to control the dogs as they barked at the prospect of an outing.

Everywhere was very still and quiet after they'd left. It was the first time Abbie had properly heard the ticking of the clock in the hall, it sounded extra loud to her ears and she realised with a shock this was also the first time she had been alone in the cottage since she had arrived.

Diana was out somewhere with Johnny who insisted on acting as her driver now he was back from Ireland. Theo was away for a few days in talks over a proposed new venture to a Pacific Island

and Sim, Abbie's heartbeat wobbled, she wasn't sure where he was.

* * *

As soon as they had driven Bethan back to the cottage from the hospital he had taken a tight-lipped leave of herself and Molly, saying he wouldn't come in as he had some urgent work to see to. Apart from a couple of telephone calls to Diana they had not seen or heard from him since.

It had been easy for Abbie to avoid being in contact with Theo as his new project meant he was away from the cottage for a few days. He and Susannah had rushed back after Bethan's accident but when the full extent of her injury proved not to be as serious as first thought, he had made another appointment with his backers and left again the next day. If he had noticed any atmosphere between himself and Abbie he hadn't commented on it.

Abbie shook her head. The estate agency had promised to update her on the flat situation as soon as something suitable came on to their books again she intended to take it. The best thing all round would be for her to move out and get on with her life.

Maybe at some future date she would look back on her time at Waterside Cottage with affection but right now her emotions were too close to the shock of finding out that Sim and Theo could be her half brothers, for her to think rationally.

Making a supreme effort to concentrate on her notes, Abbie tapped at her keyboard, resolutely shutting out all outside interruption. It was time she remembered she was a professional with a commissioned piece of work to do.

She didn't know where she stood with regard to her interview with Diana, or if Molly would give her the introductions she had promised to the other actresses she wanted to interview, but she had to work on the information she did have.

How Abbie wished she had never found the diamond brooch amongst her father's things or that Johnny Cavendish had told her that Don Foxton was probably her real father.

The back door banged to suddenly making Abbie jump. She glanced at her watch and realised an hour had passed since Molly and Bethan had left.

'Darling,' Diana laughed as she swept into the room, bringing with her the familiar scent of roses, 'how are you getting on? Have you made any progress?'

'Some,' Abbie admitted, looking up with a smile.

'Are you all alone? Where is everybody?'

'Molly and Bethan have gone for a walk.'

'Then I think I'll join them. Make Johnny some tea, will you?' She waved a hand at Abbie and disappeared as quickly as she had arrived.

With a gesture of irritation, Abbie got to her feet. She realised with a shock she had forgotten to eat any lunch and that she too was also quite thirsty. Making her way to the kitchen, she encountered a rather guilty looking Johnny Cavendish with his hands in the biscuit tin.

'Hello there,' he greeted Abbie over-heartily. 'Wasn't sure if you were going to join me. The word on the street is,' he lowered his voice, 'that you're a bit of a grump box these days. Not speaking to half the household and the other half says you snap at them for the slightest thing.'

'Sorry,' Abbie apologised yet again.

'It's my fault isn't it?' Johnny's eyes were full of concern. 'I should never have told you about Don Foxton. Damned insensitive of me. Want me to put it right with everyone and tell them what's upsetting you?'

'Best leave things as they are,' Abbie began filling the jug kettle. 'I'll be moving on shortly anyway so it won't really matter and if it's true about me, well I don't want to upset Diana.'

'As you wish. You're probably right.' Johnny put some biscuits on a plate and began looking round for milk. 'By the way,' he began as he peered into the fridge. 'Can I ask you a question?'

'Depends what it is,' Abbie replied.

'When's your birthday?'

'What do you want to know for?'

'Bit of an interest of mine, astrology. I'd put you down as a homemaker. Is cancer your birth sign? June?'

'Spot on. You have hidden talents, Johnny. Midsummer's Day is my birthday.'

'Knew it.' Johnny's smile as he looked at her was tinged with sadness.

'What's the matter?'

He seemed to pull himself together with a jolt. 'Nothing. You get the tea on. I need to send an email. Do you mind if I borrow Diana's laptop?'

'Now?'

'No time like the present.' He smiled. 'Won't be long.'

A Visitor Arrives
At The Cottage

'You know,' Theo smiled at Abbie, 'you've really put the cat among the pigeons.'

Abbie dropped the box of photos she had been going through. They cascaded over the floor. Theo was standing in the doorway, arms crossed, a sardonic smile on his face.

'It's all right,' he said noticing her look of alarm, 'I'm not coming in to help you pick them up, so there's no need to retreat behind the desk to defend your honour.'

'Theo,' Abbie affected a light laugh. 'You made me jump. I thought you were out for the day.'

'I've been having things out with Sim. I accosted him in his office and demanded to know what was going on.

234

I mean a man would have to be blind not to notice something was seriously wrong between the pair of you. I had to force him to tell me about the no contact rule he had with you and that this rule also included me. Something about us not being allowed in a room alone with you?' Theo made a face then leaned forward confidentially. 'Why's that then?' he asked. 'Have I contracted something contagious on my foreign travels and passed it on to my brother?'

Abbie cleared her throat. The sooner the agency found her a suitable flat the better. There was only so much of the family's delicate probing she could take. Why hadn't she realised that in a close community like that of Waterside Cottage everyone would be drawn into the drama between herself and Sim and that they would all want a piece of it?

'I,' Abbie made a gesture with her shoulders, 'I can't go into details.'

Theo looked disappointed. 'Well I could understand it if it was only me you wanted to ban, I can be a bit of a nuisance at times, but I usually behave if I'm slapped down. What I want to know is what's poor old Sim done to upset you? I mean Sim's a star. I know he's my brother and all that and I suppose you could say I would stick up for him, but honestly he's the best brother in the world. You won't find any better.

'Of course we have our differences, like any brothers, but at the end of the day we are always there for each other. Molly said she gave you the third degree and got absolutely nowhere so now it's my turn. What gives?'

'Sim hasn't done anything and neither have you, Theo.'

'Then why this cold war between us?'

'It's personal. Can we leave it at that?'

'No we can't,' Theo insisted. 'I thought I was doing him a favour removing Susannah from the scene and I went to a lot of trouble to arrange things on that front. I wanted you to realise Susannah wasn't the right girl for him, because she isn't. She's already got her sights on one of my production team, so there's no need to worry about anything on that score, by the way.' Theo ground to a halt.

Abbie had to clamp her hands to her sides in order not to rush across the room and hug Theo. For all his faults she loved him — as a brother, and now he was standing in front of her, smiling uncertainly waiting to hear what she had to say.

'Seems I only made things worse between the pair of you, didn't I?' Theo said. 'I am sorry. I'm not cut out for this matchmaking lark.'

'No,' Abbie shook her head at Theo. 'You didn't do anything wrong and the situation has nothing to do with you or Susannah.'

'That's a relief. You see I've always been trying to make it up with Sim after, well forever really.' He paused, looking unnaturally serious, 'you know what happened to Cathy don't you? My wife.'

'Johnny told me.' Abbie's voice was soft. 'I'm sorry.'

'It was a long time ago now. Bethan was only a baby when Cathy died in that accident with Barney.' For a moment Theo looked lost in his thoughts. 'We didn't mean to fall in love, it just happened. We agonised for ages what to do. Then we reasoned it would be worse if she went ahead and married Sim, knowing how she felt about me, so she told him she couldn't marry him. It caused a lot of upset at the time but she really was the love of my life,' Theo said.

'Sim came to realise that eventually and we all remained friends, but I've always felt I did the dirty on him by marrying Cathy. So when I realised how he felt about you I thought I could nudge things in the right direction. I'd love to see old Sim settled, so you've got no need to worry that I'll try to upset things between you, Abbie. I promise I won't.'

Abbie blinked very quickly. Molly

and Theo were two of her most favourite people in the world. She hated having to mislead them. If only she could explain things and why she was really here, but it wasn't her secret to share and in a way Sim was right, she had gained access to the house under false pretences. She didn't deserve anyone's trust or respect.

'In fact I'll be out of the action altogether soon,' Theo explained. 'I've just heard we've got the go ahead for the Pacific Project so I'll be out of the country for at least six months, possibly longer. You can congratulate me if you like.'

'That's wonderful news, Theo.' Forgetting her rigid discipline, Abbie could no longer fight the urge to put her arms round him and hug him. 'I couldn't be more pleased. When are you leaving?'

'There's no need to sound quite so delighted that I am leaving,' Theo complained, grinning back at her. 'I'm not sure about any of the details. These things always take longer than originally estimated with injections and health checks, paperwork, that sort of thing, but hopefully within the next two to three months. So you see I'm leaving the field open for you and Sim.'

'Do you mind if we don't talk about Sim?' Abbie released Theo's arm.

'Fair enough,' Theo nodded. 'I've interfered too much as it is anyway. I just wanted you to know where I stand in all this.'

They took a moment out to appraise each other. 'I haven't thanked you properly for looking after Bethan, after her accident,' Theo said. 'She sort of looks on you as a big sister.'

'I've done nothing,' Abbie protested, trying to ignore the look of gratitude in Theo's eyes.

'Yes you have. She's always talking about you. *Abbie says this and Abbie does that*. I tell you you've got quite a fan in my daughter. She's now decided she wants to be a journalist when she grows up.'

'I like her company,' Abbie admitted.

'She's a bright child and she's fun to be with.'

'Sure you wouldn't consider staying on for Bethan's sake?' Theo wheedled, then seeing the stricken expression return to Abbie's face held up a hand. 'Sorry, that was below the belt. You've got your own life to lead and the Foxtons aren't to everyone's taste, I agree. I can't blame you for wanting out. Let's change the subject.' Theo nodded at the desk. 'I'm at a bit of a loose end this morning. Want any help licking stamps on letters or anything?'

Before Abbie could reply there was a screech of outrage from the top of the stairs.

'Now what?' Theo raised his eyes in exasperation with a good-humoured smile on his face, 'honestly I shall be glad to get away from this madhouse. Give me a horde of charging rhinos any day.'

'What is this?' Diana, looking angrier than Abbie had ever seen her, flew down the stairs, her almond eyes almost on fire as she pushed Theo out of her way.

'Steady on,' Theo complained as he stubbed his toe on the doorstop, almost falling to his knees in the process. 'What do you think you're doing, Diana?'

'I'm asking Abbie what this is doing in her possession?'

Theo looked over his mother's shoulder at the diamond brooch she was clutching in her hand. Abbie swayed and grabbed on to a bookcase before her legs buckled underneath her.

'Hey,' Theo grabbed at the brooch. 'Isn't that part of the Foxton set of diamonds, the one that went missing? Yes, it is,' he said excitedly, 'I've seen enough photos to recognise it.'

'Well?' Diana ignored him, her attention on Abbie her nostrils flaring in anger.

'I . . . I . . . ' she began.

'You're not a jewel thief are you?' Theo asked. 'I mean I know there was all that nonsense about you not being the babysitter and Sim making accusations against you, but I thought we'd cleared all that up.'

'Theo, shut up.' Diana's jaw was stiff.

'Right,' Theo nodded. 'I just thought if you had your eye on the rest of the set, Abbie, you're in for a disappointment. It's in the bank under lock and key. The insurance company insisted on it.'

'Where did you get it?' Abbie asked Diana, her voice cracked and hoarse.

'It doesn't matter where I got it,' Diana retaliated, 'I want to know why you kept it hidden in your room.'

'You had no right to go through my things,' Abbie protested. She was now beginning to feel sick. Why hadn't she thought to lock her door after the first time she found Diana in her room?

'She's right you know,' Theo butted in again. 'Abbie's a guest in our house.'

'Your things?' Diana's voice rang from the rafters as she advanced towards Abbie. 'This brooch isn't yours. This brooch, as my son has pointed out, was part of a famous family collection. It went missing years ago.'

'I am not a thief,' Abbie protested.

'To think we trusted you.'

The room fell silent.

'For the baby,' Abbie said very slowly and very carefully realising there was no point in denying anything any more.

No one in the room moved. Diana's face blanched. All colour drained from her lips, then she stumbled and would have fallen to her knees if Theo hadn't leapt forward and placed a hand under her elbow.

'Diana, what on earth's the matter?'

'What did you say?' Her voice was a hoarse rasp.

Theo began to look seriously concerned. 'You don't seriously think Abbie stole the brooch, Diana? I mean she couldn't have anyway it's been missing for years. Don't you remember the insurance company being sticky over the claim? Don was always going on about the loss, saying it was your fault and you should never have left it lying around for anyone to see.'

'Are you the baby?' Diana asked.

'Sit down, Diana. You're rambling. What baby?' Theo led his mother to a chair and gently lowered her into it.

'What on earth is going on now?' No one had noticed Johnny appear in the doorway. 'Dee? You look dreadful. Aren't you feeling well?'

'She found this in Abbie's room.' Theo picked up the brooch, which had slipped from Diana's fingers, on to the carpet.

'Good lord,' Johnny gaped. 'The Foxton diamond. So I was right.' He swung round to confront Abbie. 'This is the brooch your mother gave you? The one Bethan said you showed her on the night you arrived?'

'Yes.' Abbie's shoulders sagged.

'Where did you get it?' Diana's voice was quieter now. She looked at Abbie with pleading eyes. 'Please, Abbie tell me?'

'I don't know where it came from,' Abbie said slowly and carefully.

'Then how did it get into your possession?' Theo asked.

'I found it.'

'I don't believe you,' Diana shook her head. 'You can't have done.'

'It was in an old cash box. It was wrapped in a sheet of notepaper and the writing on it said 'for the baby'.'

'No,' Diana's protest was no more than a low sob.

'The headed notepaper that was wrapped around the brooch was yours, Diana,' Abbie said. 'I knew there was a story here so I came to Waterside Cottage to try and find it out. I had to know the truth, Diana.'

'I might have guessed. I was right about you all along, wasn't I? I knew you'd come here to stir up trouble. Well, are you satisfied now?'

Sim was standing beside Johnny in the doorway, the expression on his face matching his cold voice.

'No, Sim, you don't understand,' Abbie began, unable to believe he could look at her with such loathing.

'Sim.' Theo leapt to his feet. 'What are you doing here?'

'I had an appointment with Diana. Didn't anybody look in the diary?'

'We never have done before,' Theo tried to inject a note of lightness into the room. 'Why should we start now?'

'I think I'd better take charge of that.' Sim strode into the room and held out a hand for the brooch.

'It isn't yours,' Abbie tried to snatch it from him.

'And it isn't yours either. This brooch is to be held in trust for the eldest daughter in the family. By rights it should belong to Bethan. She will inherit it when she comes of age.'

'If Abbie is who I think she is then she is the eldest daughter in the family,' Diana said slowly and carefully.

'What?' Four pairs of eyes swivelled in her direction.

'She's Don's daughter,' Diana paused, 'and Orla Dillaine is her mother.'

'What?' Sim gasped.

'I gave Orla the brooch when she told

me she was pregnant. It seemed only fair.'

'Orla Dillaine, wasn't she your dresser?' Theo asked Diana, 'the one who used to sing to me when I was at the studio?'

'Yes,' Diana smiled. 'Orla had a lovely voice.'

'And that's why the two of you fell out all those years ago, isn't it?' Johnny asked, 'because you thought she was having an affair with Don?'

'I couldn't tell you, Sim.' Abbie was looking at him. 'I only found the brooch after my father died. I had no idea my father was Don Foxton until Johnny mentioned it was a possibility the day we had lunch together in London. So you see if he is then that makes you and Theo my half brothers.'

'And that's why you've sent the pair of us to Coventry?' Theo asked.

'Yes,' Abbie replied.

Theo threw his head back and burst into laughter. 'If that doesn't beat all. Why on earth didn't you say so?'

In that moment Abbie saw Theo Foxton as he truly was. She felt sickened to think that she had believed him when he'd told her how he had fallen in love with Cathy. He was nothing but a heartless Lothario.

'How can you laugh about it?' It was all Abbie could do not to screech at him.

'Because,' Theo waved a hand at Sim, 'you tell her, Sim. It's only fair it should come from you after all it's you she's in love with.'

'No, I'm not,' Abbie's voice rose in denial.

At that moment the telephone began to ring. No one moved.

'Don't you think one of us should answer it?' Johnny asked. 'You're the nearest, Abbie.'

She still didn't move. She couldn't. Out in the kitchen she heard Molly pick up the extension.

'Waterside Cottage? Yes? Who? Where did you say you are? One moment please.'

There was the sound of her putting the receiver down on the table before she padded along the corridor, a look of excitement on her face. 'I couldn't help overhearing some of what was going on in here and I don't want to make things worse than they already are,' she began.

'Why do I suspect you're going to?' Theo asked.

'There's someone on the telephone.'

'We'd already worked that one out for ourselves, Moll,' Theo said.

'She wants to speak to you, Johnny.'

'Me?' He looked startled, then uneasy. 'Who is it?'

'Says she's at the station and would you go and pick her up.'

'Pick who up?' Johnny asked.

Molly paused looking round the room for dramatic effect. 'She says her name is Orla Dillaine.'

Abbie Meets Her Mother

The Jolly Molly swayed gently as a light breeze disturbed the evening water.

'I don't know where to start,' Orla confessed.

She and Abbie were seated opposite each other on deck, both grateful for the sensation of the cool air on their faces and the relief the evening shadow brought from the heat of the day.

From the first moment Abbie had looked at Orla she had known instinctively she was her birth mother. They were mirror images of each other. Both had a dusting of freckles across their noses, both possessed the same colour eyes and pale skin. They even had identical small moles on the side of their faces, underneath their right ear lobes.

Molly had taken charge of the situation after the pandemonium that had broken out following Orla's telephone call. She had insisted Abbie decamp from Waterside Cottage to stay on board her boat after Johnny had been deputised to meet Orla and take her straight down to the river.

'Explanations can wait and we don't want her and Diana pulling each other's hair out just yet,' Molly had announced in the tone of voice she used when she didn't want any argument on the matter.

Diana had glared balefully at Molly and then surprised everybody by agreeing with her mother.

'I'll catch up with Orla later,' she said. 'It will be lovely to see her again. But now I think I'll go and have a lie down. It's been quite an afternoon and I need to de-stress.'

'Yes well we'd all like a bit of that,' had been Molly's trenchant riposte, before seeing the stricken expression on Abbie's face. 'Off you go, darling,' she said in a softer tone of voice. 'Things will work themselves out, you'll see.

Believe me, I'm an old bird who knows about these things.

'You really should have confided in me, you know. But never mind all that now. You'll find everything you need on board The Jolly Molly. Don't hesitate to help yourself. Make yourself at home and don't even think about coming back here until the pair of you have talked everything through. You hear?'

Abbie walked down the garden to the little gate that led on to the towpath, her stomach churning, and all the while aware that most of the Foxton family were watching her progress through the large study windows.

★ ★ ★

Until recently Orla Dillaine had only been a name scrawled on the back of a faded photograph. In the space of a few days Abbie had learned she was her mother. And now she was here at Waterside Cottage. Why? What had prompted her to visit now?

Abbie glanced back at the house as she closed the riverside gate. She caught a glimpse of a shadow behind one of the curtains. She knew from the breadth of his broad shoulders that it was Sim. What was he thinking now he knew the reason why she had been avoiding him?

He hadn't spoken to her before she had left the study, and she hadn't trusted herself to look at him. How could she? He thought her sole purpose in coming to Waterside Cottage had been to get a sordid scoop on Diana's past life. It wasn't so. Abbie had only wanted the truth.

She wasn't into sensational tabloid journalism. Her interviews were more in depth, thoughtful pieces that were of interest to the majority of readers, not the lurid headline type stories that some editors preferred and no way would she forsake those principles.

Abbie's footing slipped on the damp blossom underfoot. She took a moment out to inhale the cooling scents of the river. Overhead the trees dripped after a recent shower leaving a clean green smell on the towpath.

Abbie turned her thoughts back to Diana. She must have suspected something and that was why she had gone into Abbie's room to look for the brooch. Abbie couldn't blame her even if her tactics were slightly underhand. Hadn't Abbie done more or less the same thing going through her father's belongings?

How would Diana feel confronting Orla again after all these years? By her thoughtless actions, Abbie had upset the entire family. None of them would ever speak to her again, and the knowledge that she deserved their condemnation hurt more than anything had ever hurt before in her life.

Abbie trudged on along the towpath. If there hadn't been so many witnesses to Orla's telephone call she feared she might have taken the coward's way out and refused to meet her. As it was, she had no choice. Molly would brook no refusal.

* * *

Abbie reached The Jolly Molly before Orla. It welcomed her like an old friend and the five minutes Abbie spent alone on board before Orla arrived helped calm her troubled mind.

The cake shelf was still sticky and Abbie wiped it down. Whoever had tossed it overboard had not done a very good job and bits of currants and icing had stuck hard to the surface. As Abbie scrubbed off the mess she felt as though she were cleansing a part of her own life away.

Her adoptive mother had been right in not wanting to talk about Abbie's real parents. Why hadn't she followed her example?

Abbie rinsed out her cloth and left it on the little sink in the galley. Unable to settle she tidied away a newspaper and some china. Then she opened some windows to let in the fresh air.

Every time Abbie heard footsteps down the towpath she froze, until eventually there was a hesitant tap outside and Abbie forced herself back on deck to meet the mother she had never known.

'You're absolutely beautiful. I always hoped you would be.' Orla put out a hand and stroked Abbie's hair. 'I know I've got no right to touch you, but I hope you'll forgive me?'

'What do I call you?' Abbie asked stiffly and Orla dropped her hand immediately.

'It had better be Orla, hadn't it?' she smiled. 'Your real mother was the lady who brought you up.'

'I shall always think of her as my mother, yes,' Abbie admitted. 'And her husband as my father.'

Looking at the beautiful still waif-like woman sitting opposite her, Abbie could hardly believe she was her mother. From the moment they had shaken hands Abbie had wanted to rage at her, demanding to know why she had done what she did. Strangely, she now found she couldn't.

Her father had taught her to be non-judgmental, telling her there were always two sides to every story and you never knew what had prompted a person's actions unless you had been in their shoes at the time.

'I know this must be the last thing you wanted,' Orla said.

'I suppose I brought it on myself,' Abbie replied, 'by contacting Diana in the first place.'

'That's a very generous thing to say,' Orla had not stopped smiling the whole time she looked at Abbie and she had the sort of smile that would light up the dullest day. 'Did you have a happy childhood?' she asked.

'The best,' Abbie replied.

'You don't know how it pleases me to hear you say that. A day hasn't passed without me thinking about you.'

'Why did you,' the words stuck in Abbie's throat, 'give me away?'

'I knew you'd ask that question and nothing I can say will undo what I did, so I'll be truthful with you. This is not the time for excuses. I so wanted to keep you but I couldn't. I had no money, no real home and things were different in those days. Good Irish girls did not have babies when their husbands had left them with nothing but a string of bad debts and a lot of heartache. I knew I couldn't give you a loving home environment, I really had nothing, so I did the next best thing.'

'I've never blamed you for what you did,' Abbie said, 'and my parents always said they chose me especially, so I never felt deprived.'

'Do you — understand?' Orla asked, leaning forward. 'It's a lot to expect of you. I mean I've always known who my parents were. I've got two older brothers by the way and they've got three children each so you've a ready made family. My father died last winter. You would have loved him very much.'

'What did he do?'

'He was a fisherman. He lived a simple life and he was so proud of me, his only daughter, when I set myself up in business.' Orla's generous smile lit up her face. 'You will come over to Ireland and meet us all won't you?'

'Won't your family mind?'

'They're your family too, Caitlin.'

'Caitlin?' Abbie repeated in surprise.

'Sorry, I mean Abbie. Caitlin is the name I gave you.'

'Then please still call me Caitlin. My mother called me Abbie.'

'Caitlin it is, then, and in answer to your question, times have moved on and my brothers will be delighted to have another girl in the family. They've all got sons you see. We're very short on girl power in the Dillaine family so you'll be a welcome addition. In fact they can't wait to meet you.'

'How did you find out about me and where I was! Was it Johnny?'

'He emailed me a picture of you. Says he was struck by the likeness from the moment he first saw you.'

'Everyone kept saying they thought they had met me before,' Abbie confessed.

'We are alike,' Orla agreed. 'I'm so glad we've found each other.'

'I don't think I ever would have tried to contact you,' Abbie admitted, 'if it hadn't been for the brooch.'

'Ah yes. Diana gave it to me. She said it was for you.'

'I thought you had a huge argument because of . . . ' Abbie hesitated uncertain how to go on.

'Her husband?' Orla asked quietly. Abbie nodded. 'Do you know what it's like on a set? People live so closely together, love affairs are not unusual.' Orla shrugged. 'But Diana and I didn't only argue about Don.'

'You didn't?'

'We also argued over you.'

'Me?' Abbie repeated in a daze. 'Why?'

'Before the rumours about me and Don started, I told Diana I was pregnant. She was very supportive. She

261

even offered to adopt you. She would have loved a daughter you see.'

'She said something similar when I first arrived at Waterside Cottage,' Abbie recalled, 'she even referred to me as her daughter and for a time I suspected she might be my mother. I mean why did she part with such a valuable piece of jewellery that was part of a family collection?'

'To get back at Don. When she gave it to me I had no idea that she knew what people were saying about him and me. Then when it all came out we had a huge bust up.

'I walked out on her and that was the last time I saw Diana. I'm afraid I kept the brooch because I knew it was valuable and I suppose in some strange way I too wanted to get back at Don for causing all this trouble. Then after you were born I realised how silly I had been. I could never sell a Foxton heirloom, but I couldn't give it back either, so I pinned it inside your shawl.'

'My parents must have found it when

they took me home.'

'The nurses were very strict at the home and we weren't allowed to write little notes or anything for our babies. It was heartbreaking for the girls, but the authorities insisted on a clean break but one of the nurses came from the same part of Ireland as myself and she turned a blind eye when she saw me pin the note and brooch into your shawl. She was the one who handed you over to your parents, so I knew it would stay in place.'

'I see,' Abbie said faintly.

'I'm glad your parents never showed it to you. It would only have caused trouble. It was a silly impulsive gesture but I had nothing else to give you.'

'They probably didn't realise it was as valuable as it was. Things like that meant very little to them. They were simple, dignified people. I loved them very much.'

Orla nodded gently. 'Good.'

'That was why finding the brooch was such a shock. My father was a vicar. He didn't move in the same circles as Diana. I couldn't work out the connection, so that was why I came up with the idea of interviewing Diana. I sensed there might be a story behind it. I never realised it would be my own history.'

'I'm glad you did. I would have loved to meet your family, but perhaps it was better we didn't. I might have interfered, or my presence could have upset your mother and that would have been the last thing I would have wanted to do.'

'She was a very generous person,' Abbie said, 'but she did get upset on the few occasions when I asked about you, so I stopped asking. I didn't want to hurt her.'

Orla's smile was now tinged with sadness. 'I'm sorry to cast a cloud on our reunion but one of the reasons I am here is because I also have some unwelcome news for you.'

Abbie's attention had been drawn to the little riverside bench, the one she had sat on the night of Molly's party. The night Theo had stolen Susannah away from Sim.

So much had happened since then, and all Theo's scheming had been for nothing. Orla had confirmed her father was Don Foxton. Now there was no doubt they were related.

'Sorry?' Abbie looked back at Orla. 'Did you say something?'

Orla cleared her throat. 'I've been to see my brothers and their children. They are all going to get themselves tested to be on the safe side, you see it runs in families.'

'What does?' Abbie asked perplexed.

'It's not serious but it's why I decided I had to see you after all these years.'

'Are you ill?' Abbie's raised voice disturbed some ducks nestling under the reeds. They swam in circles around the boat quacking. The Jolly Molly swayed in the swell of water they created.

'I had been feeling very tired and listless and my energy levels were down, so I went to the doctor for tests and he told me I have diabetes. It's not the serious type and it can be diet controlled, but once I knew you were definitely my daughter after Johnny emailed me your date of birth, I would never have forgiven myself if I didn't tell you of the situation.'

'So that was why he asked me my birthsign the other day,' Abbie stopped frowning. 'I wondered at the time, all that story about him being into astrology, it didn't fit somehow, but he's a very convincing fibber, I'll give him that.'

'Don't be cross with him. I wanted to be certain you were my daughter and that was the best way I could find out,' Orla said with a stricken look on her face. 'I'm not much of a mother am I, Caitlin? I've disrupted your life completely and now I've delivered some news that could change your life forever.'

'It hasn't,' Abbie smiled, 'but I'm so glad the diabetes gave us an opportunity to meet each other. Would you have come to England otherwise?'

'I don't know,' Orla admitted. 'Promise me, Caitlin, you'll go for a check up? It's very simple.'

'I don't have diabetes.'

'How can you be sure?'

'I'm a blood donor and regular checks are made.'

'You are? That's wonderful. I'm so relieved,' Orla's smile lit up her face. 'You see when I confessed everything to my brothers and their wives they absolutely insisted I had to come and tell you. They virtually had to carry me to the plane. I've never felt so sick in my life during the journey over.'

'Let's talk about something else,' Abbie said. 'Molly's given us the run of the boat for as long as we like.'

'How is she, Molly?' Orla asked.

'Same as ever. Behaving outrageously, disappearing on her bike without warning, sending everyone into a flap.'

'She's terrific, isn't she? So have you enjoyed your time with the Foxtons?'

Abbie fought down an urge to shiver. 'On and off,' she couldn't meet the questioning look in Orla's eyes.

'You can tell me, Caitlin,' Orla said. 'You never know I may be able to help.'

'I don't need help.'

'Perhaps not but something's wrong, isn't it?'

Abbie nodded after a few seconds. 'It's difficult to know where to start. Theo laughed when I told him he was my half-brother.'

'He did what?' Orla looked outraged.

'When I found out about you and Don Foxton, well before that I mean,' Abbie sighed, 'sorry I'm not making any sense. It was Sim and I actually. I was in danger of falling in love with him.'

'My dear girl that is wonderful news.'

Abbie blinked at Orla. 'What are you saying?'

'I'm sure Theo didn't mean to hurt you by laughing at you. I expect it was relief.'

'Why should he be relieved?'

'Because you're free to fall in love with Sim.'

'I don't understand.'

'He and Sim aren't blood brothers. Neither are they Diana's sons. She could never have children.'

'What?'

Abbie stared at Orla. So much now fell into place — the reason why Theo and Sim didn't look in the least alike, or have similar characters and the reason why Diana had blue eyes and Sim had golden brown ones. She wasn't his birth mother.

'It's not general knowledge. Diana didn't want the public to know, but like you they are adopted. And that was why Diana wanted to adopt you too, to make her family complete. I have to admit to my shame I wouldn't let her.'

'Because of her husband being my father?'

'My poor Caitlin,' Orla looked at Abbie with such love in her eyes, it brought a lump to her throat. 'Perhaps my coming over here was destined to be. There is absolutely no reason in this world why you shouldn't fall in love with Sim Foxton. Don Foxton is not his father and,' Orla paused, 'he's not yours either.'

'Don Foxton is not my father?'

Orla shook her head. 'That's why I was so cross about those rumours. I don't know who started them but when Diana believed them too, that was the final straw. I left, went back to Ireland and I've never been back here since — until today.'

'But,' Abbie began slowly, 'if Don Foxton isn't my father, then who is?'

Abbie's Heart Is Broken

'Airports have never been my favourite places. There's so much waiting around,' Orla confessed to Abbie. 'And would you look at that? Flight delayed.'

Orla and Abbie stared in dismay at the television screen.

'Got you girls some reading material for the journey.' Johnny bustled over from the newsstand clutching a stack of magazines and handed them to Orla. 'What's wrong?' he asked catching the look on their faces before glancing up at the departure board. 'Not more air traffic control problems?'

'Looks like it,' Abbie sighed, wondering if she had time to give Sim a quick call. She knew she was being silly but she wanted to hear his voice, if only to reassure herself that they were still on speaking terms.

'Fancy a cup of tea?' Orla suggested.

'It will help to pass the time.'

Abbie nodded. 'Good idea.'

Things had moved so fast over the past week her feet had hardly touched the ground. She and Orla had talked long into the night on the day of her arrival in England. They'd stayed on board The Jolly Molly the whole weekend until Molly had eventually come looking for them to tell them Johnny was on a cooking spree and they were expected to dinner at Waterside Cottage that evening.

When Orla had first suggested she and Abbie travel back to Ireland together Abbie had been uncertain.

'You'll be able to finish your article on Diana in peace and I'll get the boys and their families over and we'll have a real old ceilidh,' Orla had persuaded her. 'My studio is absolutely made for parties. The youngsters will make sure everything goes with a swing. Some of them are music students so we're never short of a fiddle or two and they are very inventive in their interpretations of all the classics. What do you say? We could make it an early birthday party for you?'

Molly had been up for it. 'Darling,' she said to Abbie, 'you've been through so much. You need space from us and never mind about Diana's book. It'll get done eventually. I'm sure I can manage to sweet talk the publishers into extending the deadline. It won't be the first time I've had to talk myself out of a jam.'

'If you're sure?' Abbie asked, still hesitating.

'Go for it,' had been Theo's take on the situation. 'I would invite myself along too if Sim didn't keep glaring at me and I didn't have other commitments.'

Orla had arranged everything over the internet and she and Abbie were quickly booked to fly back to Cork on the first available flight.

'Now you will keep in touch, won't you?' Johnny fussed around them like a mother hen while he sorted out a tray of tea from the buffet bar and found the two women a convenient table by the window from where they could watch the aircraft taxiing on the tarmac below. 'I don't want the pair of you disappearing never to be heard of again. I'm a bit scared Orla might spirit you away, Abbie.'

'Leave that sort of stuff for fairy tales,' Orla stirred her tea. 'Although I can't vouch for the rest of the family. I keep receiving texts on the hour every hour asking when we are arriving. Actually,' Orla took out her mobile, 'think I'll update them on the delay.'

'Of course we'll keep in touch, Johnny.' Abbie smiled into his concerned face as Orla keyed in her message. 'And thank you — for everything.'

'Am I forgiven?' He lowered his voice, not wanting Orla to overhear.

'You've done nothing wrong,' Abbie insisted.

'If it hadn't been for you,' Orla looked up from finishing her text, 'I would never have met my lovely Caitlin, here. Isn't she the most beautiful girl in the world?'

'For heaven's sake,' Abbie pleaded, laughing, 'spare my blushes.'

An easy camaraderie had sprung up between the two of them and their relationship had now relaxed into that of older and younger sister.

'She is indeed,' Johnny agreed with Orla.

He had driven them to the airport after the rest of the Foxton family had made their goodbyes.

Orla had been an instant hit with Bethan and the child had listened open mouthed to the history of the brooch, which Abbie had left in her possession, care of Diana, as the rightful heir.

'You can have it when you're grown up, darling,' Diana had promised her, 'but right now it's going to be locked away before anything else happens to it.'

'Its reappearance is going to play havoc with the insurance company,' Theo had commented, 'still, I'm sure

Diana will think up a convincing story.'

'Darling, I hope you don't think I went through your things,' Diana had explained to Abbie. 'The brooch was on the floor of your room. Something must have dislodged it from that silly hiding place you say you used. I went in to borrow your lovely blue jumper, I knew you wouldn't mind and there it was at my feet. I almost trod on it. I was so shocked at seeing it again after all these years that I acted impulsively. Goodness knows what you must have thought of me, shouting at you like a fishwife.' She raised her slender shoulders in apology. 'What can I say? I lost it, that's all there is to it, but now I really can call you my daughter, can't I?'

Abbie had hugged Diana back, too exhausted to question the logic of her last remark but pleased they were friends again.

'If you like,' she agreed with a laugh.

Orla standing to one side had elbowed them apart. 'Hey, Caitlin's my daughter.'

For a moment the two women had faced each other and everyone in the room had held their breath. The only sound was that of the kitchen clock ticking in the corner.

'How about a kiss for your old friend?'

It was Orla who first broke the silence and after that the reunion between her and Diana had been an ecstatic affair. Old enmities had been forgotten and the years had rolled away.

Now the air between them had cleared the two of them had spent the rest of the evening gossiping about the past, dredging up old stories that left them helpless with laughter and Molly declaring eventually that she couldn't take any more of their tales and stomping off to her boat for the night.

'I am sorry,' Sim had murmured in Abbie's ear, his apology drowned out by Orla and Diana's laughter. 'I shouldn't have said what I did.'

'No you shouldn't,' Abbie agreed.

'I had no idea you suspected Theo and I were your brothers.'

'I can understand that,' Abbie said, 'but you had no right to accuse me of wanting to dig up past scandals about Diana.'

'I acted impulsively.' He nodded at Diana. 'It's a bit of a family trait. I thought you had a thing going with Theo, then when you said you didn't want him touching you either, I had no idea what was going on.'

'Poor Theo.' Abbie softened. 'He thought he'd contracted a contagious disease on his travels and that I was scared of catching it.'

'No, really?' Sim's face lit up with amusement. 'You know you must be the first female in the world not to have fallen at his feet. What a blow that must have been to his pride.'

'I like Theo very much but only as a brother.'

'Let's not start on all that again,' Sim implored. 'Friends?' he asked hopefully.

'Friends,' Abbie agreed.

'So,' Sim said after a few moments of silence had fallen between them, 'you're off to Ireland with Orla?'

'That's the idea. I really do need to work on my article and she's promised to introduce me to her brothers and their families. It seemed like a good opportunity.'

Sim nodded. 'Well have a good time.'

'Will I,' Abbie swallowed, uncertain how to go on. She'd always found relationships difficult. Her last one had floundered because of her lack of commitment, but she knew if she didn't say something now, she might never have another opportunity. 'Will I see you again when I get back?'

'Of course.' Sim's reply had been carefully neutral. 'You're part of the family, aren't you?'

'Of course,' Abbie echoed, still not sure where things stood between them.

Sim had displayed no reaction to Theo's outburst that Abbie was in love with him. It was true but right now things were so up in the air, she had no idea where their relationship was going — if anywhere.

Orla's disclosure on The Jolly Molly about Abbie's real father had been the final shock of the day. She had listened in shocked surprise as Orla explained what had happened.

'We fell in love during that magical weekend at the farmhouse in Devon,' Orla said with a misty look in her eyes. 'Isn't it strange that I should have fallen in love in the county of your childhood?'

'Barney Jones, Diana's second husband was my father?'

'Of course that was before he and Diana were married.'

'Then why did he leave you?' Abbie asked.

'Because after we finished filming *Masquerade* we divorced. We were too young and I never really loved him. I couldn't tell him about you in case he demanded to take you. He wasn't really too reliable and us being together was a mistake. We decided never to speak of it again.'

'And did you never contact Barney again?'

'I thought about it but when Johnny told me Barney had married Diana, I decided the best thing I could do was to get on with my life and forget about the past.'

'And Barney really never knew about me?'

'No.'

'You have to tell Diana,' Abbie insisted. 'She still suspects Don Foxton was my father.'

'I will,' Orla promised, 'when the time's right.'

★   ★   ★

Abbie leafed through one of the magazines Johnny had provided, casting a professional eye over the style and content of the articles while Johnny and Orla chatted casually together.

'Best keep an eye on the board,' Johnny advised them. 'They don't announce departures these days and you don't want to miss your flight. In fact,' Johnny squinted at the television screen, 'you've got a departure gate. Looks like we're ready for the off.'

'In that case I'll just go and powder my nose, Caitlin. In my experience they won't be ready to board for ages,' Orla said. 'Will you wait here for me?'

Abbie nodded and began to gather together her things.

'Right then, have a safe journey.' Johnny stood up and kissed Abbie on the cheek. 'I know you'll have a good time. Take care and don't stay away too long. I'll miss you,' he added in a husky voice.

'I'll miss you too,' she squeezed Johnny's arm. 'Look after everyone, won't you?'

'That lot?' Johnny raised his eyebrows in mock horror. 'I don't think the man's been born that's up to the job, but I'll do my best.'

Abbie watched him disappear towards the lifts with a smile of affection lifting the corner of her mouth. She had a lot to be grateful for to Johnny.

'Hello there.'

A bubbly voice behind Abbie made her jump. She turned. 'Susannah?' she looked at the girl in surprise. 'What are you doing here?'

'Same as you. I'm catching a flight. Sim told me you were off to Ireland with your mother, I believe?'

'Yes,' Abbie admitted wondering when Susannah and Sim had been in contact. From what Theo had said she thought they were no longer an item.

'I had no idea you were Irish but I should have guessed with all that lovely hair. You know for a while I thought I had reason to be jealous of you and Sim. I mean you seemed to be getting on so well together. Silly of me really, wasn't it?'

'Er — what was?' Abbie asked.

'I only went off with Theo on that little jaunt because I was annoyed with Sim. We had this silly tiff over nothing really but all that is behind us now.

We're back together and,' Susannah's smile reminded Abbie of a cat about to indulge in a bowl of cream, 'we're off for a short break too, to the south of France. I managed to get a couple of last minute bookings. Everywhere is booked up right through to September and I told Sim I couldn't wait that long.'

Susannah looked round. 'Such a nuisance all these air traffic control delays, aren't they?' She frowned. 'I hope we don't have to wait too long. I am so looking forward to a few days chilling out by the pool. Sim's an excellent swimmer. Did you know?'

'No,' Abbie managed to reply, 'I didn't.'

'Well, I'd better be going. Lovely to see you again.'

'You'll never guess who I caught a glimpse of in the distance,' Orla returned to their table and picked up her bag, 'Sim — oh, sorry, did I interrupt something?' She looked across to Susannah.

'Hello,' Susannah trilled. 'You must be Orla Dillaine? I'm Susannah Green, Sim's girlfriend. I was telling Abbie we're off on holiday too, to the Cote d' Azur.'

Orla frowned. 'You and Sim? But I thought Abbie and Sim . . . ' she began.

Susannah laughed prettily. 'No. Sim was being no more than friendly with Abbie. I am sorry if you've got the wrong end of the stick, Abbie. That is so like Sim. He's so thoughtful and kind. I always have to explain things to disappointed females.

'The truth is, we've had an under-standing for ages. I admit we went through a sticky patch a little while ago, like all relationships, but we're back together now and everything's fine between us.' She glanced up at the departure screen. 'And there's our flight. Must dash. I hope you have a great time in Ireland. Sim and I will look forward to hearing all about it when you get back and I hope I'll have some news of my own too.'

She waved her ring finger in the air suggestively before rushing off towards the departure point.

Abbie watched her go feeling as if the bottom had dropped out of her world. She was in no doubt now as to where things stood between herself and Sim.

'Come on, Caitlin.' Orla chivvied Abbie into action. 'We don't want to miss our flight either and if you dare mention Sim Foxton's name to me again I might just go down to the departure gate and box him one in the eye. I am so mad you would not believe it.'

'No, Orla. I'm all right.' Abbie did her best to calm her down. 'Sim is perfectly entitled to go on holiday with Susannah. We were never an item. Susannah's right. I read too much into his kindness.'

'And you know what?' Orla didn't pause for breath. 'A little of that Susannah female would go a very long way as well. What on earth can he see in her? They say love's blind, and if she's his choice then he'd have to be.'

'Don't fuss, Orla,' Abbie pleaded, 'I am absolutely fine. Let's go and meet this family of yours, I mean ours,' she corrected herself.

'Attagirl,' Orla hugged her. 'Come on then. We haven't a moment to lose if we want to catch that plane and if the Dillaines can't cure a broken heart, then we're not the family I thought we were.'

Sim Explains His Feelings To Abbie

Abbie sat on Orla's balcony watching the sun go down on what remained of the day. Never in her wildest dreams had she imagined the Dillaine family would embrace her with such enthusiasm. From the moment she and Orla had touched down at the airport and gone through Customs, her life had been in a whirl.

'Oh, good heavens, they're all here.' Even Orla's breath had been taken away by the strength of the reception.

An enormous family party sporting decorated banners and balloons in all the colours of the rainbow were stationed in the arrivals area ready to welcome Abbie into their midst. With true Irish warmth, total strangers had joined in and the party only left the arrivals concourse when they were in danger of being ejected by uniformed officials who were rather keen to get on with the business of running their airport without the disruption of the Dillaine family intent on holding a party.

★ ★ ★

For the next week Abbie had been whisked round to all branches of the family, major and minor. Without exception they had welcomed her into their midst.

Last night had been Orla's official studio welcome party at which Abbie had been the guest of honour.

Orla's two brothers, their lovely wives and what seemed like an army of sons had not let Abbie sit out one dance.

'I've waited years to have a niece,' Orla's elder brother had said, 'so I'm not going to waste a chance of dancing with her. On your legs, Caitlin, show me what you can do.'

Abbie's feet were still aching and she was still smiling.

The students too had been as enthusiastic as the family and Abbie had received more invitations to gigs than she could possibly accept.

'I am here to work,' she had pleaded at last then laughed at the look of genuine surprise on their faces.

'No one comes to Orla's to work,' they protested.

'Caitlin does,' Orla had announced with pride. 'She's an extremely famous journalist and one day you are going to see her name up in lights alongside the big ones. Remember you heard it here first.'

Abbie had grown used to Orla's unquestionable pride and exaggeration of her achievements. It gave her a lovely warm feeling to know that someone loved her unconditionally. Her parents had loved her of course and had the same quiet pride in their daughter and it was something she sorely missed.

She sipped her soft drink to ease the

dryness of her throat. No one seemed to stop talking in Ireland and Abbie's throat muscles were beginning to react against the constant socialising.

Although this was her first visit to Ireland she knew it would not be her last.

'If you want it to be,' Orla insisted, 'this is your home. We have so much to catch up on and I never want to lose you again.'

'All my professional contacts are in England,' Abbie said, 'but I'll be over as often as possible.'

Orla's blinding smile had dazzled Abbie. Everything about Orla blinded her. Abbie had not realised quite how talented she was. Her jewellery fashioned in the traditional Celtic designs was exquisite as were her brooches and bracelets. Coach loads of visitors poured into her studio to learn about her craft and to purchase examples of her work.

Orla was down in the forecourt now sorting out a few stragglers who had been attending one of her day courses. Everyone was always reluctant to leave the studio. Orla was a professional and welcoming host and she never stinted on her time.

She waved up at Abbie as she scrambled into the driver's seat of the old van she used to make her deliveries and shuttle people to and from the nearest town.

'We won't be long, Caitlin. Get on with that article, you hear?'

'Slave driver,' Abbie called back as she got reluctantly to her feet.

She hadn't opened her laptop since she had arrived and her fingers were now itching to get to work. The enforced break had been good for her tired imagination and her subconscious had worked out a whole new angle to the series of articles she intended to write.

She sat by the open window. The sound of the sea always soothed her. In Devon the swish of the waves had been soft and gentle, here on the west coast of Ireland the sea was harsher and a more blinding blue but it still had the same stimulating effect on Abbie.

Her fingers flew over the keyboard. Writing about Diana brought back so many memories, some happy and some she would prefer to forget.

True to her word, Abbie had not mentioned Sim Foxton once since they had arrived in Ireland. She could not believe how she had been so foolish as to fall for his charm. In his own way Sim was as lethal as Theo, only Theo was more open about it. With Theo you knew exactly where you were. Not so with Sim.

Sim had been using Abbie in the same way Susannah had been using Theo. They were a pair who deserved each other, and uncharacteristically Abbie found herself hoping their French holiday was a disaster.

If Orla had not bumped into Sim at the airport, Abbie might have questioned Susannah's story about going away with him, but Orla was the last person in the world who would fib to Abbie, and if she saw Sim there, then that was good enough for Abbie.

With a swift tap of her fingers she deleted an incoming email from Sim. Susannah had probably spun him a tale about bumping into her at the airport and Abbie did not want to listen to any more excuses. That part of her life was over. What did she care about where or with whom Sim went on holiday? She had found a new family here in Ireland. Orla's brothers could not have been more welcoming. They showered her with love. She did not need the likes of Sim Foxton in her life.

An hour later the rough draft of the article was mapped out. Pleased with her work, Abbie switched off the laptop. Molly had not reneged on her promise to introduce Abbie to several of the other actresses on her list and Abbie was looking forward to meeting them. One or two she suspected might be as much of a challenge as Diana, but at least none of them would play such a significant part in her life.

Abbie glanced at her watch. Orla had been gone for over an hour and a half. It had taken Abbie a while to adjust to Orla's time clock. 'I won't be long,' could be taken to mean as little as fifteen minutes or as long as two hours. It wasn't unknown for Orla to bump into a friend and go off together for the evening.

'I've always been a free spirit,' she explained to Abbie. 'I've never had any ties so if I want to chill, then off I go. You don't mind do you?'

'I'm in no position to mind,' she replied. 'I'm the same.'

'You are?' Orla smiled. 'I suppose we do share the same genes.'

Same genes or not Abbie began to wish Orla were with her this evening. She really needed to think about getting back. Her things were still stored at Waterside Cottage, and she could not impose on Diana's generosity much longer. Then she needed to sort out somewhere to live.

A loud blast from a horn made Abbie jump. Orla's little van bumped into the courtyard and ground to a halt. She waved enthusiastically out of the window.

'I'm not stopping,' she wound down the window, 'only dropping off a delivery.'

'Orla,' Abbie called out, 'can I . . . '

'Sorry can't stop. Got a meet. Talk to you later.'

In a blur of exhaust fumes and with much crunching of gears, she exited the forecourt. As the exhaust fumes cleared, Abbie realised Orla's delivery was actually a passenger. Abbie made a gesture of frustration. Even by Orla's Bohemian standards, this was a touch over the top. What was Abbie supposed to do with the visitor? He stood in the courtyard looking up at her.

'Abbie?' he said.

It was a voice she would have recognised anywhere. It was Sim's.

Abbie swallowed. 'What are you doing here?' Her voice was a husky imitation of its usual self.

'We have to talk.'

'Why?'

'Didn't you get my email?'

'Where's Susannah?' Abbie looked round. Now the forecourt was clear again, Abbie could see there was no sign of her.

'Look, can I come up?' Sim asked. 'We can't keep calling to each other like Romeo and Juliet.'

With a reluctant nod, Abbie agreed and moments later Sim trudged through the door and into Orla's flat.

'Did Orla plan this?' Abbie demanded.

'No she didn't. She didn't know anything about it. I only sent my email after I landed. When you didn't reply I sent another one to Orla,' Sim explained as he took off his leather jacket. 'Johnny gave me her address. I got as far as the next town then well I got cold feet and began having second thoughts. Orla came to fetch me and we talked things through.'

Abbie's face hardened. 'Orla has no

right to interfere in my affairs.'

'Don't blame Orla,' Sim pleaded. 'She's only got your best interests at heart and if she's prepared to give me a chance, will you?'

The small flat seemed to shrink in Sim's presence. Feeling claustrophobic Abbie indicated the two chairs still out on the balcony.

'Shall we talk outside?'

Sim sat down in one of the chairs and faced Abbie.

'Did you have a good holiday in France?' she asked, 'with Susannah?'

'I didn't go.'

'You let Susannah down too?'

'I only gave her a lift to the airport.'

'What?'

'A detail she omitted to tell you.'

'I don't understand.'

'I wanted to say goodbye to you and have a few private words with you before you left Waterside Cottage but there was so much going on and the family kept getting in the way and before I realised it Johnny had already offered you and Orla a lift to the airport in his car.

'When Susannah telephoned me to say she was joining a friend in the south of France for a holiday and that she was leaving the same day as you, it seemed like a good idea to take her to the airport, that way I could see you off and hopefully speak to you in private.'

A shadow crossed Sim's face. 'I should have guessed Susannah might stir things up. She said she was going off to get a magazine for the journey so I hung around the departure area looking for you.

'I bumped into Johnny. Seems he saw you and Susannah talking together. By the time I tried to catch up with you you'd already gone through security and it was too late.'

'And that's it?' Abbie asked in disbelief.

'It's not a very good story I know, but it's the truth. If it wasn't don't you think I would have invented a better one?'

'Even if it is true why did you go to all the trouble of coming over to Ireland?'

'Why do you think?' Sim asked slowly.

Abbie lowered her eyes and tried to ignore the rapid beating of her heart. 'There have been enough misunderstandings between us, Sim. I'm not prepared to create any more. You are going to have to tell me.'

'I meant what I said that night down on the towpath after Molly's party.'

'What exactly did you say?'

'That I was in love with you.'

'I don't remember you saying anything of the sort,' Abbie protested, her eyes flashing into Sim's.

A slow smile stretched his face. 'Perhaps I didn't,' he agreed, 'but I wanted to.' He paused. 'Do you think you could feel the same way about me? I mean I know I'm not as charismatic as Theo . . .'

'That's nonsense,' Abbie interrupted.

'Is it?' Sim asked.

Abbie glanced across the harbour. Several moments passed before she said, 'We've never talked about Cathy.'

'No, we haven't,' Sim agreed slowly. 'It's difficult to know where to start. It was actually at our engagement party that she met Theo. I think I knew from that moment that we had no future together. They both tried to hide their feelings from me but in the end everything came out. Looking back I'm pleased it did. I lost a fiancée to Theo, not a wife and they were very happy together.'

'There's no need to go on,' Abbie said softly.

'So where does that leave you and me?' Sim asked equally softly. 'Was it true what Theo said? That you do love me?'

'I think I've loved you from the moment you offered me a bacon sandwich in the kitchen of Waterside Cottage,' Abbie admitted.

Sim raised an eyebrow. 'That late in our relationship?'

'Yes,' Abbie smiled. 'And goodness knows why, you were so rude to me.'

'That was a cover up job,' Sim admitted. 'I couldn't believe anyone as beautiful as you could fall for me, not once they'd been introduced to Theo.'

'Well I didn't fall for his charms, so where does that leave us? I'm prepared to take on your family if you're prepared to take on mine. You haven't met them yet have you — apart from Orla? Then let me tell you their parties make Foxton affairs look amateurish.'

'They don't do they?' Sim asked with a feigned look of horror.

'In fact,' Abbie turned her head to listen. 'I think I can hear some of them downstairs now. Word's probably got round already that I'm entertaining a man on the premises and they'll want to sound you out. Are you brave enough to meet them?'

'Only if you hold my hand,' Sim said with his slow smile.

'Last time you offered to hold my hand it was because you were scared of falling over on the tow path.'

'This time it's because I'm plain scared,' Sim admitted. 'How many brothers did you say Orla's got?'

'At the last count there were two and between them they've got six sons all intent on defending my honour and,' Abbie added playfully, 'you've got to face them some time.'

'Not just yet,' Sim said as he drew Abbie into his arms. 'First of all I have some unfinished business to attend to.'

THE END

We do hope that you have enjoyed reading this large print book.

Did you know that all of our titles are available for purchase?

We publish a wide range of high quality large print books including:
Romances, Mysteries, Classics
General Fiction
Non Fiction and Westerns

Special interest titles available in large print are:
The Little Oxford Dictionary
Music Book, Song Book
Hymn Book, Service Book

Also available from us courtesy of Oxford University Press:
Young Readers' Dictionary
(large print edition)
Young Readers' Thesaurus
(large print edition)

For further information or a free brochure, please contact us at:
Ulverscroft Large Print Books Ltd.,
The Green, Bradgate Road, Anstey,
Leicester, LE7 7FU, England.
Tel: (00 44) **0116 236 4325**
Fax: (00 44) **0116 234 0205**

Other titles in the
Linford Romance Library:

FOLLOW YOUR HEART

Margaret Mounsdon

Marie Stanford's life is turned upside down when she is asked to house sit for her mysterious Aunt Angela, who has purchased a converted barn property in the Cotswolds. Nothing is as it seems . . . Who is the mysterious Jed Soames and why is he so interested in Maynard's? And can she trust Pierre Dubois, Aunt Angela's stepson? Until Marie can find the answers to these questions she dare not let herself follow her heart.

A LOVE WORTH WAITING FOR

Karen Abbott

In the lovely village of Manorbier in Pembrokeshire, Jasmine gets the opportunity to open up a teashop — her dream come true. However, disturbing events threaten her business prospects, forcing Jasmine to search her heart and discover who wants the teashop closed. Is it the controlling boyfriend she has put in the past? Or someone wanting the premises for himself . . . local artist Rhys Morgan, for instance? Jasmine has to put her heart on hold until the sinister campaign is over.